Telecourse Guide
for

THE
AMERICAN
ADVENTURE

Beginnings to 1877

Telecourse Guide
for

THE
AMERICAN
ADVENTURE

Beginnings to 1877

Fourth Edition

JOHN A. TRICKEL

Produced by:

DALLAS TELECOURSES
Dallas County Community College District

An Imprint of Addison Wesley Longman, Inc.

New York • Reading, Massachusetts • Menlo Park, California • Harlow, England
Don Mills, Ontario • Sydney • Mexico City • Madrid • Amsterdam

The American Adventure is produced by the Dallas County Community College District, R. Jan LeCroy Center for Educational Telecommunications in association with the Higher Education Telecommunications Association of Oklahoma, Amarillo College, Austin Community College, Coast Community College District, Florida State Department of Education, Southern California Consortium, Tarrant County Junior College District, and in cooperation with Addison Wesley Longman Publishers.

Acknowledgments

Foremost, a special thanks to my researcher, assistant, reviewer , and friend, Carole Lester, for her immense assistance.

All books are the product of a team effort. In this case, the team members were both numerous and valued. The tireless efforts of Sandy Adams and in subsequent editions, Betsy Turner and Evelyn Wong as the editors of the telecourse guide are acknowledged and deeply appreciated. The proofreading and timely suggestions of Bob Crook, executive producer, are likewise appreciated. Sincere thanks to Theodore Pohrte for his careful attention to the details of organization and presentation. The constant, cheerful reentering of corrections by Linda Sparks is recognized. And all the other members of the Center for Telecommunications whose help made this project so meaningful, I offer my sincere gratitude.

To my family, I owe an especially great debt. So to you Rita, Erik and Brooke this work is dedicated.

—John Trickel
History Content Specialist

Funding was provided, in part, by a grant from

FRITO-LAY, INC.

Assistant Chancellor/LeCroy Center: Pamela K. Quinn
Executive Dean, Distance Education: Jacquelyn B. Tulloch
Director, Satellite Services: Robert Crook
Special Projects Consultant: Ted Pohrte
Senior Instructional Designer: Nora Coto Busby
Director, Business Services: Dorothy Clark
Video Producer/Director: Paul Bosner
Assistant Dean, Distance Education: Betsy Turner
Telecommunications Information Specialist: Evelyn J. Wong

Contents

To the Student

All people look to the past from time to time; whether through historical books or novels, old pictures, or timeless stories. Studying such records provides us with a better understanding of past generations and the problems they faced. Historians make serious, systematic efforts to study the record of the past and attempt to explain history's significance and its relation to the present. Knowledge gleaned from the past may be used to illustrate contemporary problems and provide options for solving these problems. The story of previous accomplishments and failures provides a useful yardstick by which to measure the quality of contemporary life and the success of present social arrangements.

Part of the answer to any question comes from studying the circumstances preceding it. A major role of historical study is to determine the forces, arrangements, ideas, and facts that most influenced the present condition of any given subject. The better the past circumstances are understood, the better the present results can be interpreted.

As the drama of the history of the United States unfolds in this course to the end of the Centennial, you will learn to view circumstances of the past as elements of the present. Far from being a quaint prologue to the real story, the history of the settlement of the United States and early development of American society are critically important to understanding the present.

—John Trickel

Telecourse Organization

The American Adventure is designed as a comprehensive learning package consisting of three elements: Telecourse Guide, Textbooks, and Video Programs.

TELECOURSE GUIDE

The telecourse guide for this course is:

Trickel, John, *Telecourse Guide for The American Adventure*, 4th edition. Addison Wesley Longman, 1998.

The Telecourse guide acts as your daily instructor. If you follow the Study Guidelines carefully, you should successfully accomplish all the requirements for this course. (See the section entitled, "Study Guidelines.")

TEXTBOOKS

Text: Nash, Jeffrey, et al., The American People, Volume One: To 1877, 4th edition. Addison Wesley Longman, 1998.

Reader: Trickel, John. *Perspectives on America: Volume I: Reading in United States History to 1877*. American Heritage Custom Publishing, 1997.

VIDEO PROGRAMS

The video program series for this telecourse is:

The American Adventure

Each video program is correlated with the Telecourse guide and the lesson assignment for that lesson. Be sure to read the Video Focus Points in the Telecourse guide before you watch the program. The video programs are presented in a

---

documentary format and are designed to bring analysis and perspective to the issues being discussed. Watch them closely.

If the programs are broadcast more than once in your area, or if video or audio tapes are available at your college, you might find it helpful to watch the video programs more than once or to listen to an audio tape for review. Since examination questions will be taken from the video programs as well as from the reading, careful attention to both is vital to your success.

COURSE GOALS

The successful completion of the telecourse *The American Adventure* will result in the following:

- A clear, factual understanding of the evolution of the United States from its beginnings through Reconstruction.
- An appreciation of the complex political, economic, social, and cultural heritage of the United States.
- An ability to analyze and synthesize complex historical events into meaningful concepts.
- An awareness of history as a means of reflecting and evaluating the human experience.
- A recognition of the uniqueness and impact of the American experience.

Study Guidelines

Follow these guidelines as you study the material presented in each lesson:

1. LESSON ASSIGNMENT—
    Review the Lesson Assignment in order to schedule your time appropriately. Pay careful attention; the titles and numbers of the textbook chapter, the telecourse guide lesson, and the video program may be different from one another.

2. OVERVIEW—
    Read the Overview for an introduction to the lesson material.

3. INTRODUCTION—
    To provide you with a broad thematic overview of the lesson.

4. LEARNING OBJECTIVES—
    Review the Learning Objectives and pay particular attention to the lesson material that relates to them.

5. KEY TERMS—
    Look for these people, places, events, terms, and ideas as you go through the lesson assignment. Be able to recognize them after completing the lesson.

6. TEXT FOCUS POINTS—
    To get the most from your reading, review the Text Focus Points, then read the assignment. You may want to write responses or notes to reinforce what you have learned.

7. READER FOCUS POINTS—
    To get the most from your reading, review the Reader Focus Points then read the assignment. After completing the assignment, write responses and/or notes to reinforce what you have learned.

8. VIDEO FOCUS POINTS—
To get the most from the video segment of the lesson, review the Video Focus Points, then watch the video. You may want to write responses or notes to reinforce what you have learned.

9. OPTIONAL LEARNING ACTIVITY—
These activities add to your comprehension or influence your attitude about the key historical topics in the lesson. Some instructors may accept written responses to these assignments for extra credit.

10. SUGGESTED READINGS—
The Suggested Readings are designed to encourage you to go beyond the elements required in the course.

11. HISTORICAL PERSPECTIVE—
Thoughtful questions or comments designed to stimulate and expand your interest in various historical questions.

12. PRACTICE TEST—
To help you evaluate your understanding of the lesson, turn to Appendix B and complete the Practice Test for the lesson. The Practice Test contains multiple-choice questions and essay questions, followed by a Feedback Report with correct answers and references.

Unit One
The Cultural Mosaic

1. Consequences of Contact

2. English Colonization of the Chesapeake

3. A Puritan Way

4. Diversification of the Colonies

5. The Colonial Experience

6. A New Society

7. Struggle for Dominance

The Native American cultural and social evolution in the western hemisphere was irreparably altered by the intrusion of Europeans after 1492. The Europeans conquered the lands and devastated the native tribes. In North America, France and England simultaneously built large empires. The English colonies developed social, political, and economic systems which eventually rivaled the mother country for dominance. By 1763 the English wrested control of the American continent to the Mississippi River from France, only to face a challenge from the colonists. The American settlers confronted the English authority and sought a national identity of their own.

Lesson 1

Consequences of Contact

LESSON ASSIGNMENTS

Review the following assignments in order to schedule your time appropriately. Pay careful attention; the titles and numbers of the textbook chapter, the telecourse guide lesson, and the video program may be different from one another.

Text: Nash, et al., *The American People, Volume One: To 1877*, Chapter 1, "Three Worlds Meet," pp. 4-29.

Reader: *Perspectives on America, Volume I*, "This Think Called History," by Goodrich, and "Everything You Need to Know about Columbus," by Deák.

Video: "Consequences of Contact," from the Series, *The American Adventure*.

OVERVIEW

Contact between Native Americans, Africans, and Europeans in the sixteenth and seventeenth centuries caused a tremendous upheaval in the lifestyles of these cultures. The enormous impact and consequences of these encounters is explained and analyzed.

INTRODUCTION

The people of pre-Columbian America possessed a rich and varied heritage, but their exact Asian origins and the nature of their periodic migrations to America remain shrouded in the mists of time. Archaeological and anthropological evidence, however, reveals that successive waves of these wanderers settled in the valleys and plains from Alaska to the Straits of Magellan, and from the Pacific to the Atlantic Oceans. The cultural and political institutions that arose during settlement were varied. Some settlers formed tribes of nomadic hunters and others became sophisticated agriculturalists. Some developed socialistic communities while others had despotic tyrannies. A few practiced matriarchal leadership while others had patriarchal ascendancy. Regardless of any social, cultural, or political feature, contact with the white gods on wings of the wind proved catastrophic to native societies.

Like the American tribes to the West, the ancient and varied peoples of Central West Africa were irreversibly affected by contact with Europeans. The rich cultures of black Africans were decimated by nefarious slave trade practices and abominable economic policies of Africans and Europeans alike. European contact forever altered the black heritage that once had existed.

Europe in the fifteenth through eighteenth centuries was undergoing a transformation from an obscure and insignificant power in world affairs to a dominant one. The European transition began in response to economic interests awakened by contact with near-Eastern traders in the aftermath of the Crusades. The demands of trade eventually wore away many of the Medieval bonds of localism and barter and replaced them with national monarchies and capitalism. Traditional intellectual ideas weakened and were soon challenged by the ideas of the Renaissance and Reformation. Europeans aggressively sought the riches of the world, spurred on by the conviction of their religious and cultural superiority.

These dynamic forces propelled the explorers of Portugal and Spain to heights of conquest and glory, bringing in their wake the destruction and annihilation of the Native Americans. Because of Christopher Columbus's explorations, a whole world of possible conquests lay before the Europeans. Spain was the first country to seize opportunities in the Americas. By the mid-sixteenth century, Spaniards had established large and wealthy colonies.

The consequences of Spanish colonization stretched far beyond the rampant inflation and social unrest their acquisition of huge quantities of silver and gold caused in Europe. The conquests overwhelmingly transformed the human, plant, and animal life of both hemispheres. Diseases and maltreatment devastated a vast population of natives. Ancient ways of life were destroyed. But new plants were introduced to the lands and domesticated animals soon roamed new homelands from Argentina to the Hudson Bay. A whole environment was ravished, and then transformed by the conquerors. Europeans adopted American goods, such as corn, potatoes, beans, tobacco, and chocolate. Europeans also used the Americas to produce prodigious quantities of valuable crops brought from Africa and Asia, like sugar and coffee.

The modern American cultures that emerged from the contact between Europeans and natives were the ultimate consequences of contact. And the experiences of the Europeans and natives began the American Adventure.

LEARNING OBJECTIVES

Upon completion of this lesson you should develop and be able to demonstrate an understanding of:

1. The conflicts between these three cultures in the late fifteenth and early sixteenth centuries:
   A. The Native American settlers
   B. The West African populations
   C. The Europeans
2. The nature and consequences of exploration and colonization sponsored by Portugal and Spain to 1600.
3. The consequences of the contact between European and native cultures in the Americas.

KEY TERMS

Look for these items as you proceed through the lesson assignments. Be able to define them upon completion of this lesson.

People

Ferdinand of Aragon	Vasco da Gama
John Calvin	Martin Luther
Isabella of Castile	Juan Ponce de Leon
Christopher Columbus	Montezuma
Vasquez de Coronado	Opechancanough
Hernando Cortés	Francisco Pizarro
Bartolomeu Diaz	Hernando de Soto
Prince Henry the Navigator	

Continued on next page

Places

Aztec Empire
Brazil
Genoa
Kingdom of Ghana
Inca Empire

Kingdom of Mali
Pisa
presidios
Venice

Events and Terms

Archaic Era
Beringian Epoch
depletion of megafauna

Post-Archaic Period
Reformation
Renaissance

Ideas

Elect
Justification by Faith

Predestination
environmental devastation

TEXT FOCUS POINTS

The following focus points are designed to help you get the most from the text. Review them, then read the assignment. You may want to write notes to reinforce what you have learned.

Text: Nash et al., *The American People*, Chapter 1, pp. 4-29.

1. What do the life experiences of Opechancanough reveal about the nature of European and native contact?
2. Where did the first Americans actually come from? What stages of development had these cultures undergone before the arrival of Columbus?
3. What does the map on page 6 demonstrate about the relationship between the Ice Age and migration to the New World?
4. What were the major contrasting world views between Native Americans and Europeans of the fifteenth century?

---

5. What were the varied cultural characteristics of African societies by the fifteenth century?
    A. The Kingdom of Ghana?
    B. The Islamic Kingdom of Mali?
    C. The lesser Kingdoms?
6. According to the map on Figure 1-4, page 16, what were the areas of European-African contact? What were the major Products and the areas of their acquisitions?
7. What were some shared characteristics of fifteenth century African people?
8. What forces were transforming the Europeans of the fifteenth century and preparing them for four centuries of expansion?
9. What were the roles and contributions of the Portuguese in European colonization?
10. What did Columbus expect to find by sailing West? What were his contributions to exploration?
11. Using the map on Figure 1-5, page 21, what were the routes and discoveries of the major explorers from Diaz to La Salle?
12. Who and what was at the center of the religious conflicts of Europe in the sixteenth century? What role did these conflicts play in colonization?
13. Who were the conquerors and the conquered in the sixteenth century Spanish expeditions into America? What primary crop developed in the Portuguese Colony of Brazil?
14. What were the significant biological and economic results of the Spanish conquests of the 1500s?
15. What were the Spanish interests in the conquests of North American Territory?

READER FOCUS POINTS

Reader: *Perspectives on America, Volume I*, "This Think Called History," by Goodrich, and "Everything You Need to Know about Columbus," by Deák.

1. What are the main focal points of effective understanding of history?
2. What are the main interests of a historian?

3. What did Columbus actually achieve in 1492? What did he intend to accomplish? What did he initially claim?
4. How did Columbus go about his voyage?
5. What did Columbus bring back from the New World? What did he leave behind?
6. How did he view the natives? What happened on his third and fourth voyages?
7. What kind of man was Columbus?

VIDEO FOCUS POINTS

The following focus points are designed to help you get the most from the video segment of this lesson. Review them, then watch the video. You may want to write notes to reinforce what you have learned.

Video: "Consequences of Contact"

Synopsis: Addresses the vast and varied consequences of contact between Cortés and Native Americans.

1. How did the political, economic, and social organization of the Native American peoples affect Spanish conquests?
2. What major forces were influencing Spain to become involved in colonization?
3. What elements did the historian Gary Nash suggest made conflicts between these cultures likely?
4. Why did Cortés's contact with the Aztecs evolve into a vicious war of conquest? Why was Cortés victorious?
5. What were the consequences of the Spanish conquests for Spain? The Native Americans? Other Europeans? The American environment? Which of these consequences did Professor Nash emphasize?

OPTIONAL LEARNING ACTIVITIES

1. Research the natives who settled near your hometown prior to European contact. Write a two-page evaluation of their lifestyle and how contact with European settlers changed them.
2. Historians have learned to use the tools and findings of many other disciplines to help explain the past. One discipline that has provided considerable insight for historians is archaeology. After reading pages 10-11 in the text, explain in a two-page essay what you have learned about the value of archaeology for understanding American history. How has archaeology increased our knowledge and understanding of Native American culture and history?

SUGGESTED READINGS

Further readings can be found in the text on page 35.

HISTORICAL PERSPECTIVE

Two key ingredients that drastically altered the Americas after European contact were deadly microbes and prolific plants and animals. How might European colonization have been different if the natives had not been so susceptible to European diseases? How might modern world food supplies be different without the integration of new and old world food sources? How did these foods alter world population growth? How important were these features of the contact of the old and new Worlds? Should these experiences be considered as the modern world begins the conquest of outer space?

PRACTICE TEST

To help you evaluate your understanding of the lesson, turn to Appendix B and complete the Practice Test for the lesson. The Practice Test contains multiple-choice questions and essay questions, followed by a Feedback Report with correct answers and references.

Lesson 2

English Colonization of the Chesapeake

LESSON ASSIGNMENTS

Review the following assignments in order to schedule your time appropriately. Pay careful attention; the titles and numbers of the textbook chapter, the telecourse guide lesson, and the video program may be different from one another.

Text: Nash et al., *The American People, Volume One: To 1877,*
Chapter 1, "Three Worlds Meet," pp. 30-34; and
Chapter 2, "Colonizing a Continent," pp. 36-48.

Reader: *Perspectives on America, Volume I,* "Jamestown Fiasco," by Morgan.

Video: "English Colonization of the Chesapeake,"
from the series, *The American Adventure.*

OVERVIEW

The Chesapeake regions that were the cradle for the first permanent English settlements in America are the settings for an examination of its early colonization. The difficulties in establishing political, social, and economic order in this environment are explored.

INTRODUCTION

England's modest colonial endeavors virtually ceased following the death of Henry VII in 1509. For nearly a century, England's internal political, religious, and economic instability prevented further English exploration of the New World. Not until Queen Elizabeth's reign (1558-1603) was enough political, religious, and economic stability established that colonial activities were again possible.

The renewed efforts at colonization were funded by private or joint capital ventures. The motives to colonize were varied and complex. The desire to reap a profit certainly influenced many colonizers. Others pursued religious goals, and most felt their place in England's social order was threatened. The colonial leaders and investors came from the landed gentry, nobility, and merchants who were encountering significant problems caused by inflation. Following them to the colonies were the urban unemployed and displaced tenant farmers. The England of the late sixteenth and early seventeenth centuries was indeed vexed and troubled. Exploration and colonization was believed to be a cure for many of the problems, but attempts to colonize were unsuccessful at first. English efforts did not take hold until the early 1600s.

In December 1606, more than 100 English passengers boarded three ships bound for the New World. After a circuitous, four-month voyage, the passengers arrived at their new homeland weary, but hopeful. They settled Jamestown, Virginia, the first permanent English settlement, in 1607. Financing for the new colony came from the Virginia Company.

The Jamestown experience proved that colonization would not be easy, nor would it bring instantaneous wealth. In their eagerness to find immediate wealth, the colonists failed to prepare adequate food and housing to survive the winter. By spring 1608, two-thirds of the colonists had died. New settlers soon arrived, but many of those died as well.

Stability was an elusive goal for these early English settlers. Their hopes for rapid settlement and great wealth were quickly dashed by the hard facts of life in the New World.

The economic and political development of Jamestown came slowly and painfully. But by 1622, profits were being made by the growing and selling of tobacco, local representatives formed a House of Burgesses, and the colony's population grew. This promising beginning was dramatically slowed by a severe Indian uprising in 1622. The natives were defeated, and a truce was arranged, but the Virginia Company was destroyed. Virginia became a direct possession of the King in 1624.

Once the colony became a possession of the monarchy, the first royal colony, development quickened. Settlers poured into the colony by the thousands. The population neared 20,000 by 1660, although the death rate remained high.

Across the Chesapeake from Virginia, a colony was created in the 1630s as a refuge for English Catholics. Its founder, Lord Baltimore, had many dreams, but the harsh reality of the American environment stymied his endeavors. The religious policy of the colony by 1660 was toleration of both Catholics and Protestants.

After overcoming initial set-backs, these Chesapeake colonies experienced rapid economic growth, but they remained politically and socially unstable. Political and social developments were retarded by the incessant death rate and lack of effective leadership. Family life was difficult for several reasons. The sex ratio remained overwhelmingly male. The death rate was high; on the average, adults died in their forties. The frequent death of spouses resulted in remarriages and large families with many half-siblings. Children had only a one-in-two chance of reaching five years of age. And, the institutions of church and school made very limited progress in this youthful society.

Despite the obvious problems in this unstable society, it attracted thousands of settlers. The odds might be long, they reasoned, but the possibility of owning large tracts of land unhampered by feudal restrictions seemed worth the risk. The rewards for the fortunate English settlers who survived were significant. The society lacked the refinements and institutional stability of England, but it provided opportunities for people from all strata of English society.

LEARNING OBJECTIVES

Upon completion of the lesson you should develop and be able to demonstrate an understanding of:

1. The motives and reasons for English exploration and colonization in the late sixteenth and early seventeenth centuries.
2. The slow and difficult evolvement of colonial settlement in Virginia and Maryland to 1660.
3. The unstable and tenuous nature of social, political, and economic institutions in the Chesapeake to 1660.

KEY TERMS

Look for these items as you proceed through the lesson assignments. Be able to define them upon completion of this lesson.

People

Lord Baltimore	Philip II
John Cabot	Pocahontas
Coastal Algonquians	Powhatan
Elizabeth I	Sir Walter Raleigh
Sir Humphrey Gilbert	John Rolfe
Henry VIII	John Smith
Mary I	John White
Opechancanough	Jamestown

Places

Roanoke	Maryland
Virginia	defeat of the Armada

Events and Terms

indentured servants	joint-stock company

Ideas

fragility of life	social and institutional instability

TEXT FOCUS POINTS

The following focus points are designed to help you get the most from the text. Review them, then read the assignment. You may want to write notes to reinforce what you have learned.

Text: Nash, *The American People*, Chapter 1, pp. 30-34; and Chapter 2, pp. 36-48.

1. What were England's initial interests in the far side of the Atlantic?

2. What changes were occurring in England in the late sixteenth century that propelled the English into overseas exploration and colonization?
3. Why were the first English attempts at colonization feeble and ill-fated? What changes were made in financing and organization to enhance the chances for success?
4. What prompted English people to be involved in colonial activities either as colonists or investors?
5. What ideas and information about the Native Americans did the initial English settlers have?
6. What were the resources for the Roanoke settlement? What happened to the settlement?
7. What was a joint-stock company? What role did the Virginia Company play in colonization? Why did colonists go to Jamestown?
8. What was the relationship between the early Virginia settlers and the natives?
9. Using the map on figure 2-2, page 41, where was Jamestown located in relationship to the present United States? Where were the major Native American villages in the Powhatan Confederacy?
10. Despite the many hardships, what discovery started Virginia toward prosperity? How did the company fill the need for more settlers/laborers?
11. How did the demands of a tobacco culture increase friction with the natives?
12. Why and by whom was the colony of Maryland developed?
13. Why was the family center of the Virginia society a very fragile institution? How was this fragility of society characterized in other developments?

READER FOCUS POINTS

Reader: *Perspectives on America, Volume I,* "Jamestown Fiasco," by Morgan.

1. What were the major mistakes and disasters that befell Jamestown from 1609 to 1618?
2. What accounts for these gross errors and mistakes?
3. What was the nature of the governor's rules for the colony after 1610?
4. What one ray of hope existed for the colonists after ten years in Jamestown?

VIDEO FOCUS POINTS

The following focus points are designed to help you get the most from the video segment of this lesson. Review them, then watch the video. You may want to write notes to reinforce what you have learned.

Video: "English Colonization of the Chesapeake"

Synopsis: Addresses the difficulty of establishing an English society in the Chesapeake environment.

1. Why were the early English colonizers real "risk-takers"?
2. What were the expectations and dreams of the settlers?
3. What factors propelled England into colonial activity?
4. What was the "starving time"? What did it teach the settlers and the company?
5. What elements of change in organization and development occurred by 1622 that helped Jamestown survive?
6. What three things did the prosperity of Jamestown require?
7. What did Professor Edmund Morgan propose as the reasons for Jamestown's survival?
8. Why did English institutions have difficulty being transferred to America?
9. How was family life destabilized by the seventeenth century Chesapeake environment?
10. What factors did Professor Morgan give for the difficulty of transplanting English society?

OPTIONAL LEARNING ACTIVITY

Read a more detailed account of the early years of Jamestown (i.e. relevant chapters from Alden Vaughn's *American Genesis: Captain John Smith and the Founding of Virginia;* or chapter 4 of Edmund Morgan's *American Slavery: American Freedom* found in *Perspectives on America, Volume I,* "Jamestown Fiasco." Upon completion of the reading, write a two-page paper on why Jamestown faltered so

---

badly at first, and what was learned from those experiences that was used to improve later settlements.

SUGGESTED READINGS

Further readings can be found in the text on pages 68-69. Of special interest is *American Slavery: American Freedom* by Edmund Morgan.

HISTORICAL PERSPECTIVE

People are more comfortable when they feel secure and life seems stable. The living experiences of people in the seventeenth century Chesapeake environment were anything but stable. Life was hard, and frequently saddened by the death of loved ones. Institutions such as churches and schools rarely operated effectively. The economic opportunities were undermined by overproduction and sharp price reductions, thus making income uncertain. And the political authority of the leaders was challenged by a variety of forces. This multitude of forces helped create the American society of the seventeenth century. In wrestling with these difficulties, the settlers created a truly "American character." Speculate on what characteristics this new society would come to prize most highly and how those values would be different from their "English habits."

PRACTICE TEST

To help you evaluate your understanding of the lesson, turn to Appendix B and complete the Practice Test for the lesson. The Practice Test contains multiple-choice questions and essay questions, followed by a Feedback Report with correct answers and references.

Lesson 3

A Puritan Way

LESSON ASSIGNMENTS

Review the following assignments in order to schedule your time appropriately. Pay careful attention; the titles and numbers of the textbook chapter, the telecourse guide lesson, and the video program may be different from one another.

Text: Nash et al., *The American People, Volume One: To 1877,* Chapter 2, "Colonizing a Continent," pp. 48-57.

Reader: *Perspectives on America, Volume I*, "Indians in the Land," by Cronon and White.

Video: "A Puritan Way," from the series, *The American Adventure.*

OVERVIEW

The craggy seashore, the glaciated land, and the New England village provide the visual background for a look at the experiences of Puritan settlers to 1660. The reasons for the mass migration of English Puritans to New England from 1630-1660 are explored, along with the results. The objectives, successes, and ultimate disintegration of their "Wilderness Zion" are the issues studied.

INTRODUCTION

The Puritans wanted to reform the Church of England into a truly Protestant body. Puritan opposition to state control of their local churches peaked as Charles I took the throne in 1625. His desire to return state control to the state church further alienated the Puritans. His "high church" preferences and Catholic-like policies

---

brought vigorous reactions from the Puritans. The Puritan-dominated House of Commons confronted the king on two issues: his marriage to a French Catholic and his taxation policies. The resulting conflict convinced thousands of devout Puritans to leave England. Many came to the shores of Massachusetts as the Separatist Pilgrims had a decade earlier.

The Puritans received a charter from the government to settle in America. The charter helped establish a governing pattern which allowed them to select their own leadership. The Puritans took the royal charter for the Massachusetts Bay Company to America to make it more difficult for the king to interfere with their intended lifestyle. The New World afforded them the opportunity to create a social order based on their ideals.

The Puritans believed in a strict Protestant theology. The belief that God knew and foreordained all things was the foundation of their theological system. Those who were destined for salvation were already determined; the rest were to be consigned to damnation. The Puritans believed the selected ones, called the elect, could generally be recognized by their moral behavior. These special "Children of God" were to assume the roles of community and church leaders and rule in light of God's law as found in the Bible. Such a community would be a "city on a hill," a living testimony to godly life. This gave the Puritans purpose and direction in their colonial endeavors. They demanded conformity from all of those who participated in the settlement. Although the laws were rigid and harsh, they created close-knit human communities of like-minded people.

The Puritans suffered fewer of the economic and human hardships that affected the Virginia colonists because the Puritans had sound financing, greater numbers, and good preparations. The leadership demanded carefully planned and controlled expansion. Each new town was formally created by the Massachusetts General Court and had to provide adequately for the economic and spiritual needs of its members. The land was divided and worked according to old English customs. The lack of a significant cash crop resulted in more economic diversification within the towns than was typical in the Chesapeake colonies. But as the population grew, struggles over opening new fields and settlements erupted in conflicts that were anything but holy.

Uncertainty was a part of Puritan life, even though their convictions carried them through many hard times. Certainty eluded them even when they experienced a sense of God's saving grace, for no one knew God's will for sure. The most intimate human relationships were viewed with suspicion as a possible trap of Satan. Despite such doubts, they lived very human lives. They drank their ales, and celebrated weddings with gusto. They were sexually active and had large families. In short, they were typical country English people trying to live by the ideology they espoused. Failure to meet their ideals fully was inevitable; that they accomplished so much is a monument to their dedication. The Massachusetts Bay Colony grew and prospered. But the original intensity of purpose waned as the towns grew and second and third generations came to power. Lament as they may, the ethic of hard work, thrift, and godly service tended to make wealthy, self-satisfied citizens. The Puritan Way had succumbed to the Yankee spirit.

LEARNING OBJECTIVES

Upon completion of the lesson you should develop and be able to demonstrate an understanding of:

1. The reasons for the founding of a Separatist colony in Plymouth and a Puritan colony in Massachusetts.
2. The plans for the development of an economic and political system in the Massachusetts Bay Colony.
3. The social, political, and economic tensions of colonial settlement in New England.
4. The reactions of the Puritans to dissent.
5. The problems and accomplishments of the Puritan settlers.

KEY TERMS

Look for these items as you proceed through the lesson assignments. Be able to define them upon completion of this lesson.

People

William Bradford	Pequots
Charles I	Wampanoags
Anne Hutchinson	Roger Williams
James I	John Winthrop

Continued on next page

Places

Boston

Harvard

Massachusetts Bay Colony

Plymouth Plantation

Plymouth, Massachusetts

Rhode Island

Events and Terms

closed field system

Confederation of New England

covenant

elect

General Court

Massachusetts Bay Company

Mayflower

open field system

Pilgrims

Puritan

Separatist

Ideas

antinomianism

"calling"

separation of church and state

"work ethic"

TEXT FOCUS POINTS

The following focus points are designed to help you get the most from the text. Review them, then read the assignment. You may want to write notes to reinforce what you have learned.

Text: Nash et al., *The American People*, Chapter 2, pp. 48-57.

1. How did the Puritans want to change the Church of England? What did they distrust about the changes in English society?
2. Why did the Puritans come into conflict with James I and Charles I?
3. Who were the Separatists? Why was their colony significant?
4. What did the Puritan settlers of the Massachusetts Bay Colony hope to accomplish?

5. What did the Puritans accomplish? What problems and tensions did they endure? How did they deal with dissenters like Roger Williams and Anne Hutchinson?
6. From the map on page 52, what were the four official colonies of New England? Where are they located in relationship to the modern Atlantic coast of the United States?
7. What kind of relationship did the Puritans establish with the Indians? With what result?
8. What was the role of the village in Puritan life? How did it help create a vastly different society than in the Chesapeake? Contrast the two societies.
9. Why did the Massachusetts Bay Colony population increase so rapidly? How did the life span of these settlers compare with Chesapeake settlers? What vital role did women play?
10. How was literacy and education another binding element of Puritan society?
11. What was the reason for the establishment of the Confederation of New England?

READER FOCUS POINTS

Reader: *Perspectives on America, Volume I*, "Indians in the Land," by Cronon and White.

1. How have historians interests and perceptions of environmental factors in American history changed in recent years? How has this interest altered our understanding of Indians?
2. How did seasonal changes affect Indian people? How did European diseases alter the practices of various tribes? How did the horse change their lifestyle? How did trade for European goods affect them?

VIDEO FOCUS POINTS

The following focus points are designed to help you get the most from the video segment of this lesson. Review them, then watch the video. You may want to write notes to reinforce what you have learned.

Video: "A Puritan Way"

Synopsis: Addresses the reasons for the mass migration of English Puritans to Massachusetts and the results.

1. Why did many Puritans feel a sense of urgency to immigrate during the reign of Charles I?
2. What did they hope to establish in the New World? How did these hopes reflect English unrest? Their religious views?
3. What was the role of the village in Puritan life?
4. How did the community deal with dissenters like Anne Hutchinson?
5. What did Professor Edmund Morgan say were the successes and failures of the Puritans?

OPTIONAL LEARNING ACTIVITIES

1. In a two-page essay, discuss what you found most and least admirable about the Puritans. What traditions and ideas developed in New England had the most significant impact on later American development?
2. Read the "Recovering the Past," article in the textbook pages 46-47. In a two-page paper, explain what can be learned by studying the type of housing common to an area and a time. In comparing the housing patterns of colonial New England and Chesapeake, what differences existed in the seventeenth century? How can those differences be explained?

SUGGESTED READINGS

Further readings can be found in the text on pages 68-69. Of special interest is *The Puritan Dilemma: The Story of John Winthrop* by Edmund S. Morgan.

HISTORICAL PERSPECTIVE

Today the term "puritanical" is associated with strict, humorless, prudish, intolerant, and anti-intellectual behavior. Which of these characteristics really seems to apply to the settlers of New England? What is your explanation for their adoption of those particular attitudes or policies? Which of these characteristics are least indicative of seventeenth century New England Puritans? Has your view of the Puritans been changed by what you have learned? Explain.

PRACTICE TEST

To help you evaluate your understanding of the lesson, turn to Appendix B and complete the Practice Test for the lesson. The Practice Test contains multiple-choice questions and essay questions, followed by a Feedback Report with correct answers and references.

Lesson 4

Diversification of the Colonies

LESSON ASSIGNMENTS

Review the following assignments in order to schedule your time appropriately. Pay careful attention; the titles and numbers of the textbook chapter, the telecourse guide lesson, and the video program may be different from one another.

Text: Nash et al., *The American People, Volume One: To 1877*,
        Chapter 2, "Colonizing a Continent," pp. 57-68; and
        Chapter 3, " Mastering the New World," pp. 70-82.

Video: "Diversification of the Colonies,"
        from the series, *The American Adventure*.

OVERVIEW

The rich diversity of Philadelphia, the patterned simplicity of the Pennsylvania Dutch country, and the lush rice regions of South Carolina set the visual tone for an analysis of the changing character of American colonization into the early 1700s. The purposes, hopes, and experiences of founders and followers are examined.

INTRODUCTION

English colonial activities changed dramatically after the restoration of the English monarchy in 1660. The return of the king followed 20 years of turmoil and a brief period of Puritan rule. The new ruler, Charles II, used English colonial lands much differently. He granted huge claims to various individuals and groups who would then hold the lands as proprietors. These proprietors encouraged immigration and settlement for many reasons.

New York was granted to Charles II's brother, James, the Duke of York. Carolina was granted to a group of aristocratic friends of the king. The two colonies shared many economic and political features. The New York grant was designed to consolidate English control of the previous Dutch colony of the New Netherlands and to enrich the Duke.

Therefore, the colony was organized by traditional, English landholding policies with huge estates designed to be worked by rent-paying peasants. This system brought few long-term settlers to New York with so much available land elsewhere. Carolina was similarly established using policies outlined by the philosopher John Locke. Carolina filled the labor needs through indentured servants and, later, black slaves. Carolina evolved a rigid class structure with aristocrats and slaves. Its wealth was concentrated in rice production and its social system was based on racism and slavery.

The colony of Pennsylvania was the result of the dreams of William Penn and King Charles II's debt to Penn. Penn was a convert to the Society of Friends, or Quakers, a radical religious sect. He envisioned his American possession as a place to live and work in peace and liberty. Penn intentionally sought immigrants from various German states and provinces. Thousands flocked to Pennsylvania. By the 1720s the "Pennsylvania Dutch" possessed small farms stretching far to the west and north of Philadelphia. Although they rarely paid their rents to the proprietor, they lived on their small farms growing good crops of grain and practicing their religion without being disturbed by the authorities. Many other peoples immigrated to Pennsylvania, each adding to the diversity, and each finding a place to seek their dreams.

To this mixture of European immigrants was added the forced migration of enslaved Africans. The experience of the black African had several divergences from indentured white migration. The concepts of indenture, which initially were applied to Africans, were soon replaced by an increasingly rigorous system of racial slavery. The black experience began with capture, continued through a process of transactions and forced passages, and ended at an auction block in the New World. Their bondage was permanent and transmitted to all of their progeny. Their rights as people were generally ignored and the profits of their labor were garnered by others. The slave experience in South Carolina was especially harsh due to the dangers and rigors of the rice plantations. Slavery was a system of economic exploitation and social control which left an indelible mark upon the American society. The Africans

---

eventually created a black culture within the slave experience; a culture that reflected not only the reality of their status, but also their dreams and rebellions.

Diversity and accommodation contributed significantly to the evolvement of an eighteenth-century American society. The ethnic, religious, and social diversity of American settlers gave the legal, political, and economic institutions adopted from England new dimensions. Such ideals as one church-one state seemed totally inappropriate. Pennsylvania stood as proof that divergent religions and nationalities could live peacefully within one political system. South Carolina revealed that through exploitation of black labor, great profits could be extracted from southern agriculture. As a whole, the English colonies showed remarkable diversity and individuality, forming societies with varying degrees of unity and weak ties to any central political or religious authority. This immense pluralism had significant consequences for the evolving society.

LEARNING OBJECTIVES

Upon completion of the lesson you should develop and be able to demonstrate an understanding of:

1. The impact of the restoration of the English monarchy on the American colonies.
2. The goals, approaches, and results of the proprietors who owned the colonies of New York and Carolina.
3. The establishment of Quaker colonies, with special emphasis on the development of Pennsylvania.
4. The similarities and differences in the development of the late seventeenth century proprietary colonies.
5. The evolvement of slavery in the American colonies, and its relationship to the economic environment where it was introduced.
6. The development of a black culture within the slave experience.

KEY TERMS

Look for these items as you proceed through the lesson assignments. Be able to define them upon completion of this lesson.

People

Charles II

Delaware Indians

James, Duke of York

Anthony (Antonio) Johnson

John Locke

William Penn

Susquehannocks

Popé

Places

Carolina

Holland

Hudson River

New Netherlands

Pennsylvania

Philadelphia

West Jersey

Events and Terms

black codes (slave codes)

middle passage

slave trade

Society of Friends (Quakers)

staple crop

Idea

"inward light"

TEXT FOCUS POINTS

The following focus points are designed to help you get the most from the text. Review them, then read the assignment. You may want to write notes to reinforce what you have learned.

Text: Nash et al., *The American People*, Chapter 2, pp. 57-68; and Chapter 3, pp. 70-82.

1. What were the economic and colonial policies of Holland in the first half of the seventeenth century?
2. Why and how did England challenge Dutch control of the New Netherlands? With what results?
3. Who were the proprietors of Carolina? Why were they given the colony? What were their plans for the colony?
4. How did Carolina actually develop? What happened to the Indians?
5. How did the northern part of the Carolina settlement differ from the southern lowlands? With what results?
6. What made the Society of Friends, or Quakers, seem so radical in the seventeenth century?
7. Where and why did the Quakers first settle in the English colonies?
8. What were William Penn's plans for Pennsylvania? How did he deal with the Indians? With what result?
9. How were Penn's plans changed by the reality of settlement in his colony? How did the colony reflect the later development of the United States?
10. How did the life of Anthony Johnson show the changing nature of slavery in seventeenth century America? How did his life and family show that slavery was becoming more rigid?
11. Why did the African slave trade begin? When and why was it expanded to the Americas?
12. From an analysis of the map on page 73 and the graph on page 74, what were the origins, destinations, and numbers involved in the African slave trade from 1526-1810?
13. What was the slave trade like?

14. When and why were Africans introduced to English North American colonies? Why did the numbers and usages increase in the late seventeenth and early eighteenth centuries?

15. What were the uses for slaves in the North? What role did northern commerce play in slavery?

16. How did the legal organization and status of Africans evolve from 1619 to 1700?

17. How and why did the slaves develop their own cultural and social systems? What were the characteristics of those systems? How did they vary from place to place?

18. In what ways did slaves resist their bondage?

19. What were the roles of religion and family in English American slavery?

20. What were the problems the Spanish encountered in the frontier outposts in Florida and New Mexico?

VIDEO FOCUS POINTS

The following focus points are designed to help you get the most from the video segment of this lesson. Review them, then watch the video. You may want to write notes to reinforce what you have learned.

Video: "Diversification of the Colonies"

Synopsis: Addresses the contrast of motivation and experience of the settlers who came to Pennsylvania and South Carolina.

1. What was the Quaker vision? How did Penn try to make that vision a reality in America? How successful was he?

2. What made cultivation in Carolina so difficult and dangerous to health? What was the eventual solution to the lack of laborers?

3. What myths about slavery hid its true nature? What was different about slavery in the Americas?

4. According to Professor Gary Nash, what influenced the growth and development of slavery in South Carolina?

5. Why did so many Germans migrate to Pennsylvania in the early eighteenth century?
6. What role did diversity play in the evolution of "America" according to Professor Nash?

OPTIONAL ACTIVITY

In a two-page essay, describe the experiences of an African who was captured, transported, and auctioned into North American slavery. To personalize the experience, write the essay in the first person as if you lived it!

SUGGESTED READINGS

Further readings can be found in the text on pages 68-69, and pages 98-99. Of special interest is *Quakers and Politics* and *Red, White and Black* by Gary Nash.

HISTORICAL PERSPECTIVE

The modern United States is a vast pluralistic society with an enormous variety of people, religions, and ideas. The diversity which is associated with modern America began in the late seventeenth century. How did the experiences of colonial governmental leaders, like those in Pennsylvania, undermine the previous assumptions about the need for unity of church and state? What other seventeenth century assumptions about political, economic, and social arrangements were undermined by these pluralistic realities? How was it possible for the country to accommodate such a wide variety of social roles?

PRACTICE TEST

To help you evaluate your understanding of the lesson, turn to Appendix B and complete the Practice Test for the lesson. The Practice Test contains multiple-choice questions and essay questions, followed by a Feedback Report with correct answers and references.

Lesson 5

The Colonial Experience

LESSON ASSIGNMENTS

Review the following assignments in order to schedule your time appropriately. Pay careful attention; the titles and numbers of the textbook chapter, the telecourse guide lesson, and the video program may be different from one another.

Text: Nash et al., *The American People, Volume One: To 1877*,
           Chapter 3, "Mastering the New World," pp. 82-98.

Video: "The Colonial Experience,"
           from the series, *The American Adventure*.

OVERVIEW

The settings include a southern tavern and the fences and fields of New England. The colonists' experiences in English America as they continued to pursue land, freedom, and opportunity for themselves are analyzed. These experiences included systematically removing Indians from their lands, facing internal dissension among themselves, and resisting English demands to conform to the needs of empire.

INTRODUCTION

The American colonists continued to experience numerous conflicts and difficulties during the last half of the seventeenth century. As a result of working through these problems, American colonists became wary of England's motives and jealously guarded their economic and political rights.

One recurring problem was the conflict between westward-moving settlers and Native Americans. King Philip's War, a violent upheaval between white New Englanders and local natives, erupted in 1675. The New Englanders suffered destruction of several towns and the loss of hundreds of lives. But the Indians suffered the destruction of most of their villages and thousands of their people. This was the last notable New England-Indian war, although fear of additional warfare kept the settlers edgy for years to come.

A confrontation between whites and Indians in the 1670s in Virginia was more complex than previous conflicts and involved broad political and economic issues. The governor refused to support the plans of frontier settlers to attack local tribes in reprisal for an Indian attack on some whites. This refusal precipitated a crisis between the Indians and whites, and among the whites themselves. Frontier Virginians found a leader in a young, impetuous, and recently-arrived Englishman named Nathaniel Bacon. Bacon not only killed Indians without regard to their previous hostility, he also rebelled against the governor. Bacon's Rebellion, though violent, did reflect several features of most colonists' concerns: their fear of Indian warfare; their unhappiness with Governor Berkeley's policies; and the divergence between local and English interests in the colony. The rebellion may have ended with Bacon's death, but repercussions were felt for many years as the colony continued to grow and expand. The hatred of Indians during this period became a feature of life in Virginia that remained for years to come.

Conflict was not limited to Indian warfare. The colonists also were directly affected by English attitudes toward America and its organization. English attempts to control America created hostility between the Americans and the English.

King Charles II wanted to increase royal control over the colonists' trade and political systems, but never managed to get an effective plan implemented. His brother, King James II, made a grandiose attempt. He combined northern colonies into a single Dominion of New England under the absolute governorship of Edmund Andros. While Andros struggled to subdue the American colonists, James II was forced from the monarchy and into exile. This so-called Glorious Revolution brought Parliament into dominance and the monarchy into the hands of William III and Mary. When the king's governor, Andros, was unceremoniously kicked out of Boston and returned to England, King William did not punish the colonists. Other upheavals were put down and royal control was reestablished. However, the nature and intent of that influence was significantly altered. The ruling motivation now seemed to be to maintain enough trade and political control to guarantee an English profit, but at the least possible cost.

From the late 1690s until the 1750s, the restrictions on American political and economic behavior remained, but were systematically ignored by both American and English officials. This period of "salutary neglect" had major repercussions in the mid-eighteenth century.

Throughout this period the colonists not only faced external threats, they also turned inward and fought each other. The most sensational incident was an outburst in Salem Village, Massachusetts. Twenty people were killed in an outbreak of witchcraft hysteria. The incident was a symbol of the deep and abiding hostilities in colonial society.

In the late 1600s American colonists became involved in the conflicts between England and its European enemies on the North American continent. A series of wars convulsed the New World beginning with King William's War in 1689 and lasting until the end of the French and Indian War in 1763. The colonists were called upon to provide soldiers and material. The Americans provided as little support as possible, except when their own settlements were threatened.

Although the colonies of England were firmly planted and many settlers prospered, the colonial experience remained tenuous and difficult.

LEARNING OBJECTIVES

Upon completion of the lesson you should develop and be able to demonstrate an understanding of:

1. The nature, results, and effects of late seventeenth century Indian wars on the natives and white settlers.
2. The relationship of the American colonies to England following the changes in English colonial administrative policies and the Glorious Revolution.
3. The significance of England's wars to the American colonists.

KEY TERMS

Look for these items as you proceed through the lesson assignments. Be able to define them upon completion of this lesson.

People

John Alden	Narragansetts
Edmund Andros	Samuel Parris
Nathaniel Bacon	Ann Putnam
William Berkeley	Thomas Putnam, Jr.
James II	Susquehannocks
Jacob Leisler	Tituba
Queen Mary	Wampanoags
Metacomet (King Philip)	William of Orange

Places

Dominion of New England	New France

Events and Terms

Bacon's Rebellion	Papists
Glorious Revolution	Peace of Utrecht
King Philip's War	Queen Anne's War
King William's War	the rabble

Ideas

war for extermination	witchcraft

TEXT FOCUS POINTS

The following focus points are designed to help you get the most from the text. Review them, then read the assignment. You may want to write notes to reinforce what you have learned.

Text: Nash et al., *The American People*, Chapter 3, pp. 82-98.

1.   What triggered King Phillip's War? What was at the root of the difficulties? What were the results of the conflict?
2.   What were the primary issues involved in Bacon's Rebellion? What did Bacon do in response to the Indian "problem"? What were the results of the conflict?
3.   In what ways had England attempted to regulate the American possessions in the seventeenth century?
4.   What precipitated the Glorious Revolution?
5.   What was the Dominion of New England? What happened to it during the Glorious Revolution?
6.   What happened in New York following the Glorious Revolution?
7.   What were the general colonial results of the Glorious Revolution?
8.   What characteristics of social order did the American colonists try to achieve? With what success?
9.   What were the main ingredients that allowed the Salem witchcraft incident to get out of hand? What does it reveal about the nature of colonial social order?
10.   What position had France achieved in the New World by 1690? What were the causes and results of conflicts between France and England to 1713?
11.   What were the results of the colonial experience by 1715?

VIDEO FOCUS POINTS

The following focus points are designed to help you get the most from the video segment of this lesson. Review them, then watch the video. You may want to write notes to reinforce what you have learned.

Video: "The Colonial Experience"

Synopsis: Addresses the instability and uncertainty of the colonial experience as a result of Indian conflicts, the Glorious Revolution, and witchcraft.

1. What did King Philip's War seem to indicate about white-Indian relationships?
2. What did Nathaniel Bacon and his supporters want to do about the Indian "problem"? In pursuing his policy, what happened in Virginia?
3. What results of Bacon's Rebellion did Professor Gary Nash note?
4. Why was Edmund Andros resented in the colonies? With what result?
5. Why did the years of the Glorious Revolution seem like troubled times in the American colonies?
6. What significance did Professor Edmund Morgan give for the period of the Glorious Revolution?
7. What does the witchcraft episode indicate about colonial New England?
8. What explanation and interpretation of the witchcraft incident did Professor Morgan provide?

OPTIONAL LEARNING ACTIVITIES

1. The witchcraft outbreak in Salem has long fascinated historians. In a two-page essay, assess what forces might explain the hysteria and support an analysis of why it took place.
2. One frequently overlooked resource for studying history is a cemetery. Attitudes about success, religion, and social status can be gleaned by studying tombstones. What do the two illustrations in the textbook, pages 86-87, reveal about changing attitudes in New England from the late seventeenth to the late

eighteenth centuries? What do modern cemeteries show about contemporary attitudes concerning death, burial, and society?

SUGGESTED READINGS

Further readings can be found in the textbook on pages 98-99.

HISTORICAL PERSPECTIVE

The need to establish a sense of order and stability is at the heart of many of the colonists' problems. In what ways had they met failure in trying to establish political and social order? If they continued to fail in their attempts to create a proper society, what alternatives did they have? Could such experiences possibly lead them to question the conventional wisdom of political and social affairs? What new ideas were generated from these experiences?

PRACTICE TEST

To help you evaluate your understanding of the lesson, turn to Appendix B and complete the Practice Test for the lesson. The Practice Test contains multiple-choice questions and essay questions, followed by a Feedback Report with correct answers and references.

Lesson 6

A New Society

LESSON ASSIGNMENTS

Review the following assignments in order to schedule your time appropriately. Pay careful attention; the titles and numbers of the textbook chapter, the telecourse guide lesson, and the video program may be different from one another.

Text: Nash et al., *The American People, Volume One: To 1877*, Chapter 4, "The Maturing of Colonial Society," pp. 102-142.

Video: "A New Society," from the series, *The American Adventure.*

OVERVIEW

A bustling seaport, a thriving college, and a legislative chamber visually symbolize the evolving economic, intellectual, and political culture of the English colonies. All were instrumental in the development of a uniquely American character.

INTRODUCTION

The trauma of seventeenth century settlement helped produce a mature and diverse society in the eighteenth century. By the middle of the eighteenth century, an identifiable American society and culture had emerged. The population became more ethnically and racially diverse as immigrants arrived by the thousands. The birth rate remained high and the southern death rate began to decline. The increase in population was so rapid that the number of colonists doubled every twenty-five years.

The economic and political developments of the colonies were no less startling. The British attempts to reorganize the empire politically (see telecourse guide Lesson 5) were paralleled by policies for economic reorganization. At the heart of English imperial policy was the assumption that the empire was created and maintained to benefit the Mother Country's merchants, sailors, and officials. The means of measuring the success of their policies was the accumulation of wealth. The best means for accomplishing this goal was to establish a "favorable balance of trade." These so-called mercantile policies were carried out in a series of navigation acts passed sporadically from 1650 to 1750. The laws were designed to direct the colonists' trade into the proper British channels. To many American colonists, the laws were unfair infringements on their rights to make a living. Until the 1760s, the informal arrangement was for the English authorities to laxly enforce the laws (salutary neglect). The colonists evolved several different patterns for economic prosperity from within this formal-informal framework.

The variation in regional production and habits of trade resulted in several identifiable patterns under mercantile policies. The New England colonies discovered that their agricultural production was suitable for local exchange, but entering the Atlantic economic community required extensive trade.

The middle and southern colonies produced agricultural commodities for specific markets. The middle colonies grew grain and traded with southern and Caribbean producers. Southern producers grew staple crops geared to the English market. In fact, they provided England with 75 percent of its American imports, yet found themselves deeply in debt to British merchants and bankers.

Besides the evolving patterns of economic divergence, powerful new intellectual commitments were being formed. The Great Awakening was one event that transformed the colonists. This religious reaction to growing secularism was promoted throughout the colonies in the 1730s and 1740s by ministers like Jonathan Edwards, George Whitefield, and Gilbert Tennent. The "new light" converts developed strong anti-authoritarian feelings as they grappled with the "old light" leaders. This religious enthusiasm permeated the society, creating a united group of converts who viewed life and society in a specific way. Their sense of unity and purpose took precedence over their loyalty to local authorities, colonies, and England.

The rationalism of the Enlightenment was another intellectual current that affected the educated colonists. Although primarily a movement influencing a small core of the elite, these ideas and attitudes frequently penetrated the common citizen's thoughts through popular publications such as *Poor Richard's Almanack*. The ideas of natural law and deistic religion were commonly expressed to the populace. The Awakening and Enlightenment influenced the American understanding of politics, life, and society. These perceptions called English policies and authorities into question and later precipitated strong resistance.

Colonial societies also had undergone political alterations. Each colony adopted the forms of English Parliamentary government with an executive (the governor), a two house legislature, and a judiciary (court system). But the real power to rule rested in the hands of the legislative lower house. The lower houses had the power to tax and controlled the governors' salaries. Frequent disputes with the governors left the colonists with strong reservations about executive authority and experience in ways to control it. Additionally, a relatively large percentage of white adult males could vote. These factors combined to give colonial political institutions a somewhat different shape than their English model.

The society which had evolved and was functioning by 1750 in North America had undergone significant alterations. Clearly the modes of thought and ways of life differed markedly from England. This new society later challenged the English authorities and created a new country.

LEARNING OBJECTIVES

Upon completion of the lesson you should develop and be able to demonstrate an understanding of:

1. The results of the population increase and the economic systems which evolved in each region of the colonies.
2. The mercantile system and the implications of its application to the American colonies.
3. The nature, impact, and significance of the Great Awakening and the Enlightenment.
4. The political relationships of England to the colonies, and the political organization of the colonies.

KEY TERMS

Look for these items as you proceed through the lesson assignments. Be able to define them upon completion of this lesson.

People

James Davenport
Jonathan Edwards
Benjamin Franklin
John Hancock
Thomas Hancock

John Locke
Scots-Irish
Gilbert Tennent
John Peter Zenger

Places

Atlantic basin
middle colonies

New England
southern colonies

Events and Terms

artisans
Board of Trade
bicameral
Enlightenment
Great Awakening
gentry life style
half-way covenant
indentured servant

indigo
mid-wife
new lights
old lights
Poor Richard 's Almanack
rice culture
secularism
Whig (republican) ideology

Ideas

40-shilling freehold
Old Colonial system

mother-centered family

TEXT FOCUS POINTS

The following focus points are designed to help you get the most from the text. Review them, then read the assignment. You may want to write notes to reinforce what you have learned.

Text: Nash et al., *The American People*, Chapter 4, pp. 102-142.

1. What were the reasons for the rapid population growth in the colonies during the first half of the eighteenth century?
2. Using the maps on page 106, what were the locations of the greatest concentration of Scots-Irish and German settlements by 1775?
3. What was the social background of most of the eighteenth century immigrants to the colonies?
4. What were conditions like for indentured servants and black slaves?
5. What impact on trans-Appalachian natives did the influx of white settlers have in the mid-eighteenth century?
6. What were the characteristics of the French presence in the trans-Appalachian region? the Spanish?
7. How did the French and Spanish view Colonial inhabitants of mixed race? What effect did their policies have on local cultures?
8. What were the characteristics of northern agriculture? Why did many New Englanders turn to trade or move west?
9. How were values changing in northern colonies? How did Franklin exemplify these changes? How were women's roles changing?
10. What ecological changes occurred due to the arrival of the Europeans into the trans-Appalachian area?
11. What were the characteristics of the tobacco culture? The rice coast? Frontier farming?
12. How were family and sex roles different in the eighteenth century American society? How did these roles vary between planters and small frontier farmers?
13. What were the functions of colonial urban society?
14. What were the roles of American merchants in the Atlantic basin trading system?

---

15. What part did artisans play in the colonial towns? What were the emerging social structures and value system?
16. What was the "American Enlightenment"?
17. What were the messages, leaders, and results of the Great Awakening?
18. What were the elements (formal structures) of government in the English political system? Who participated in English government? What was the role of the crowd in colonial governance? Which element (structure) of government came to dominate the American political system?
19. What were the elements of "Whig" or republican ideology? What was the role of the press in spreading these ideas?

VIDEO FOCUS POINTS

The following focus points are designed to help you get the most from the video segment of this lesson. Review them, then watch the video. You may want to write notes to reinforce what you have learned.

Video: "A New Society"

Synopsis: Addresses the transformation of English economic, intellectual, and political traditions into and American society.

1. How was trade binding the Atlantic world together?
2. According to Professor John Trickel, what were the dominant trade/economic patterns of colonial America?
3. What other urban class was emerging? What attitudes were developing?
4. What was the Great Awakening? What were the roles of Jonathan Edwards and George Whitefield?
5. What were the roles of religion in eighteenth century life, according to Professor Trickel? What effects did the Awakening have on the colonists?
6. What were the elements of colonial government?
7. How did American experience and Whig ideology change political attitudes, according to Professor Trickel?

OPTIONAL ACTIVITY

Read The Recovering the Past section, pages 126-27 on sermons. Write a two-page analysis of what they were saying, why people reacted to them as they did, and what role such sermons played in New England life.

SUGGESTED READINGS

Further readings can be found in the text on pages 142-143.

HISTORICAL PERSPECTIVE

A major element in understanding the emergence of the American Revolution was the development of an "American character." The colonists' experiences with political and economic affairs caused them to deviate from the English model in several ways. The colonial political system was more open and fluid, which led to new assumptions about how a proper society functioned. The colonists designed economic patterns primarily to increase their profits. What alterations in social ideals were necessitated by their experiences with pluralism? What attitudes about church and state resulted from religious diversity? What other areas of life were impacted by colonial conditions and what happened because of these conditions? What were the key characteristics of the "American character"?

PRACTICE TEST

To help you evaluate your understanding of the lesson, turn to Appendix B and complete the Practice Test for the lesson. The Practice Test contains multiple-choice questions and essay questions, followed by a Feedback Report with correct answers and references.

Lesson 7

Struggle for Dominance

LESSON ASSIGNMENTS

Review the following assignments in order to schedule your time appropriately. Pay careful attention; the titles and numbers of the textbook chapter, the telecourse guide lesson, and the video program may be different from one another.

Text: Nash et al., *The American People*, Volume One: To 1877, Chapter 5, "Bursting the Colonial Bonds," pp. 144-177.

Reader: *Perspectives on America, Volume I*, "Verdicts of History: The Boston Massacre," by Fleming.

Video: "Struggle for Dominance," from the series, *The American Adventure*.

OVERVIEW

Events at Fort Niagara, in Boston's polite neighborhoods, and at Boston Harbor all played a significant role in the struggle for control of the North American colonies. The French-English conflicts decided which European nation would have to deal with the colonists' demands for control of their society. The deterioration of American-British relationships following the French-Indian War and the American protests of British policies propelled the colonists toward independence.

INTRODUCTION

The definitive conclusion to the French and Indian (Seven Years') War significantly altered the balance of power and brought to the colonists a renewed awareness of the vulnerabilities as well as the advantages of being English. The conflict had begun in the Ohio Valley over the establishment of French forts. At its end, this far-flung conflict ended French power in North America.

The colonists' euphoria over victory was quickly overwhelmed by the reality of postwar problems. The English government faced several key problems including a massive war debt, the administration of territories dominated by foreign citizens, and a change in national leadership. The predominant issue was the economic crisis. English citizens groaned under heavy taxes while the colonists paid relatively low ones. George Grenville, the new Prime Minister, arranged to have new mercantile acts imposed on the colonists in an attempt to alleviate England's economic burden. The Sugar and Currency Acts of 1764 were protested against but grudgingly accepted. But in 1765,when Grenville announced a stamp tax for the colonies, the colonists became defiant and bitter. This direct revenue measure required official stamps on deeds, wills, newspapers, marriage certificates, and tobacco.

A Stamp Act Congress met at New York and protested by petition. More direct and violent actions were taken elsewhere. A mob in Boston attacked the home of the town's designated stamp seller and later the homes of Vice Governor Hutchinson and others. Parliament acquiesced, and the law was repealed four months after it began. But American suspicions of England and English disgust with the colonists intensified.

The British government in 1767 passed a series of indirect taxes suggested by the Chancellor of the Exchequer, Charles Townshend. Some British officials foolishly believed that these small import duties on numerous everyday items would be accepted because they were indirect taxes. The colonists protested vehemently the use of these internal taxes to pay for the administration of an Empire over which they had little influence and in which they had no representation. For two years the protests continued. The Townshend Duties were repealed in 1770 (except for a three cent tea tax) because Americans boycotted British goods. Prime Minister Lord North decided to have the other duties repealed as a gesture of goodwill. News of the repeals even helped diffuse the anger in the colonies over the Boston Massacre which occurred the same spring.

The calm following the repeal of the Townshend Duties was shattered with the passage of the Tea Act in 1773. The law was designed to aid the financially-ailing East India Company. The law gave the British company a monopoly on all tea shipped to the American colonies. The company also was exempted from paying duties in and out of England. The act caused a storm of protest in America. The colonists objected to a monopoly on shipments to America. They also believed it was a way to trick them into paying the illegal tea tax. No British East India tea was successfully landed and sold in the American colonies. The most famous incident was the destruction of the India tea in the harbor at Boston. The Boston Tea Party so outraged King George III and Lord North that they pushed a series of punitive acts through Parliament. These so-called Intolerable (Coercive) Acts met stiff resistance in the colonies. The defiant colonists called a protest meeting for the fall of 1774 in Philadelphia. The First Continental Congress took only moderate actions. But the American colonists were uniting in opposition to British policies.

During the next year and a half, events accelerated toward a violent collision of views. Colonial militia and British regulars battled at Concord and Lexington, which injected a powerful new emotional force into the conflict. The Second Continental Congress met and appointed George Washington to command the troops, then wrote an explanation to the King for taking up arms. The King responded with a Proclamation of Rebellion followed in a few months by Parliament's Prohibitory Act, which excluded American trade from the Empire. In the spring of 1776, Thomas Paine's pamphlet, *Common Sense*, stirred many to support independence. The die was cast. War was at hand!

LEARNING OBJECTIVES

Upon completion of the lesson you should develop and be able to demonstrate an understanding of:

1. The nature and consequences of the French and Indian War.
2. The reasons for England's new mercantilistic policies and the colonists' reactions to them.
3. The varied reactions of different regions and people to the confrontations with Britain.

KEY TERMS

Look for these items as you proceed through the lesson assignments. Be able to define them upon completion of this lesson.

People

John Adams	Thomas Jefferson
Samuel Adams	Ebenezer MacIntosh
James Braddock	Alexander McDougall
Cherokee Indians	Andrew Oliver
George Grenville	Thomas Paine
George III	William Pitt
John Hancock	Chief Pontiac
Patrick Henry	Charles Townshend
Thomas Hutchinson	James Wolfe
Iroquois Indians	

Places

Fort Duquesne	Fort Niagara
Louisbourg	Quebec

Events and Terms

Boston Massacre	Molasses Act, 1733
Boston Tea Party	nonimportation
Common Sense	Proclamation of 1763
Currency Act, 1764	Sons of Liberty
Declaratory Act, 1766	Stamp Act, 1765
Declaration of Independence	Sugar Act, 1764
East India Company	Tea Act, 1773
Intolerable (Coercive) Acts	Townshend Acts (Duties)
Massachusetts Circular Letter	

Ideas

Direct and indirect taxes	Inalienable rights

TEXT FOCUS POINTS

The following focus points are designed to help you get the most from the text. Review them, then read the assignment. You may want to write notes to reinforce what you have learned.

Text: Nash et al., *The American People*, Chapter 5, pp. 144-177.

1. What conflicts had erupted between England and France involving the American colonies before 1754? What were the results of these conflicts?
2. Where and why did war break out between England and France in the mid-1750s?
3. What roles did Native Americans play in these imperial wars? How did these activities change the natives' cultures?
4. Why and how did the British eventually win the French and Indian War? What resulted from this win?
5. What problems faced Britain in the postwar period? What did George Grenville propose to do and what resulted from his actions?
6. What were the Townshend Duties? Where were the protests most significant? What methods finally got a change in the taxes?
7. After the repeal of the Townshend Duties, what action by England brought on the next crisis? What were the colonists' responses to it?
8. What were the Intolerable Acts? How did the Americans respond to them initially?
9. Why did the British march on Concord and Lexington? What resulted from the march?
10. What was Common Sense? What was its significance?
11. What were the main points of Jefferson's Declaration?
12. What new ideas were emerging in America in regards to republicanism and revolution? How were these ideas disseminated?
13. What various revolutionary roles were played by urban citizens? What roles were played by women and farmers?

READER FOCUS POINTS

Reader: *Perspectives on America, Volume I*, "Verdicts of History: The Boston Massacre," by Fleming.

1. What is the gist of what happened on the cold March day in 1770s Boston, now called the Boston Massacre?
2. Why did John Adams and Josiah Quincy consent to defend Captain Preston and the soldiers? What actions did Samuel Adams (John's distant cousin) take before the trial? What actions did the commanding general, Thomas Gage, recommend?
3. How did Governor Hutchinson postpone that trial?
4. What surprise did John Adams spring at the first arraignment? In the subsequent trial of Captain Preston, what strange events led to his acquittal?
5. How was the soldiers' trial different than Preston's? What evidence was given as to motives for the conflict? What were the tactics of the defense and the outcome of the trial?
6. How had John Adams aided the liberty movement and perhaps saved Samuel Adams?

VIDEO FOCUS POINTS

The following focus points are designed to help you get the most from the video segment of this lesson. Review them, then watch the video. You may want to write notes to reinforce what you have learned.

Video: "Struggle for Dominance"

Synopsis: Addresses the disintegration of relations between the American colonies and the English government following the French and Indian War.

1. What were the major consequences of the French and Indian War for the English? French? American colonists? Native Americans?
2. Why did the colonists object to the new mercantile policies of England, according to Professor Edmund Morgan?

---

3. Contrast Tory and radical views over disturbances in Boston concerning the Stamp Act.
4. What was the Tea Act? What were American reactions to it?
5. What factors did Professor Morgan say led to hostilities between colonists and English authorities?

OPTIONAL LEARNING ACTIVITIES

1. Beginning with the article from the reader, "Verdicts of History: The Boston Massacre," by Fleming, assume that you are a lawyer for the defense at the trial of the soldiers involved in the Boston Massacre. How was the soldier's trial different than Preston's? What evidence was given as to motives for the conflict? What were the tactics of the defense and the outcome of the trial? Research the trial record (one convenient source is a reader by Becker and Wheeler, *Discovering The American Past: A Look at Evidence*) and decide on your strategy. Write a two-page brief for the defense.
2. Carefully read and analyze the Recovering the Past sections of the textbook on pages and 154-155. Write a two-page paper analyzing the differences between the economic profile of the town and county populations on the tax records, and the social differences from the household inventories. What other uses could be made of this data? Develop a thesis to explain the increased social hostility in 1760s-1770s America.

SUGGESTED READINGS

Further readings can be found in the text on pages 176-177. Of special interest is *The Stamp Act* by Edmund S. and Helen Morgan and *The Urban Crucible* by Gary B. Nash.

HISTORICAL PERSPECTIVE

Civil disobedience and mob actions were a common occurrence during the 1765 to 1773 period of colonial history. The English authorities generally chose to take mild or conciliatory actions. The English reactions to the Boston Tea Party were different. Why did the English government choose to take a much harder line? Based on an analysis of the Intolerable (Coercive) Acts, what could the colonists anticipate? What options remained for Boston? The other colonists? If the colonists decided to reject the actions of England, what could England do? Did the Intolerable Acts make war inevitable?

PRACTICE TEST

To help you evaluate your understanding of the lesson, turn to Appendix B and complete the Practice Test for the lesson. The Practice Test contains multiple-choice questions and essay questions, followed by a Feedback Report with correct answers and references.

Unit Two
The Revolution Secured

The declaring of independence was only a first step in the securing of a republican United States. A war was fought for the rights of the white residents to govern themselves. Independence forced the creation of new governments in each state, and a minimal central authority was formed. The weak confederacy of the United States, after considerable turmoil, was replaced by the stronger central organization created by the Constitution of the United States. The domestic and foreign threats to the survival of the country dominated the affairs of state until a second war with England ended in 1814. During the following decade, the United States consolidated its political place in the world and became a bustling, growing, and strengthening country.

Lesson 8

A Revolution for Independence

LESSON ASSIGNMENTS

Review the following assignments in order to schedule your time appropriately. Pay careful attention; the titles and numbers of the textbook chapter, the telecourse guide lesson, and the video program may be different from one another.

Text: Nash et al., *The American People, Volume One: To 1877,* Chapter 6, "A People in Revolution," pp. 180-202 (end at "Ferment of Revolutionary Politics").

Reader: *Perspectives on America, Volume I,* "Triumph at Yorktown," by Rudolph.

Video: "A Revolution for Independence," from the series, *The American Adventure.*

OVERVIEW

The success of seemingly disorganized and untrained American civilian armies is followed through events in New York City, Trenton, Saratoga, and Yorktown. Brought into focus is the nature of the conflict between the United States and England and the people who fought the war.

INTRODUCTION

The odds in favor of the Americans winning their independence seemed remote indeed. The high-toned philosophy of natural rights and political liberalism which permeated "radical republicanism" was poorly suited to sustaining a long war. The difficulty of creating even the meager central government established by the Articles of Confederation forecast the problems of maintaining united actions. The United

States appeared destined for a short stay on the historic stage.

Initial military efforts of the young country did little to quiet the fears of failure. George Washington took command in the summer of 1775. After the British evacuated Boston, Washington decided to defend New York City the following summer. This decision was a disaster. Washington was out-maneuvered and ran from the area in a forced retreat. As he prepared winter quarters for 1776-77, his disheartened army began to melt away. In a gamble, Washington broke winter camp, invaded New Jersey, captured the Hessians at Trenton, and fought the regulars to a standstill at Princeton. Militarily these battles were insignificant, though unremarkable; but for the morale and confidence of Washington's troops they were critical engagements. His dispirited men revived, and he had an army for the next summer's campaign.

The conflict's turning point came during September and October 1777 in upstate New York as the Americans responded to an ambitious British campaign. The three-pronged English drive through New York state was intended to snuff out the revolution in a single stroke. Instead, one of the British armies, invading from the Lake Erie region, was stopped in western New York. Another, dispatched from New York City toward Albany, was recalled by General William Howe, who pursued his own plans. A cocky third force marching slowly south from Canada under the command of General John Burgoyne was met and defeated at Saratoga in October. This stunning reversal provided the French with an excuse to recognize the claim of the United States to independence. America's war for independence was now an international struggle between old and bitter enemies.

As the war continued, Washington's army survived a grueling winter of deprivation at Valley Forge, Pennsylvania, as well as inconclusive battles and the monotony of campaigning. The main theater of combat shifted to the South in 1778. There the British won many battles, a few impressively. But final victory was elusive. The British regulars and American loyalists could win engagements, but once the army was gone, they could not retain control of the countryside. In short, they were winning the battles but losing the war. The culmination of this campaign came when General Charles Cornwallis retreated to the peninsula of Yorktown, Virginia. By shrewd and quick actions, Washington confronted the British general with overwhelmingly superior forces. The French navy blockaded Cornwallis's planned sea escape. The chagrined general surrendered his army to this rebel planter. The news of Cornwallis's surrender forced Lord North's government out of office. When the new English government came to power it began serious negotiations. A peace treaty was completed at Paris in 1783. The war was over, but the effects were to linger for decades to come.

The war brought profound changes to the country. Deep divisions between loyalists and rebels left scars. The economy suffered, and many lost their jobs. Old patterns of trade were disrupted, and new ones needed to be established. Family ties were broken, and marriages delayed. The war caused massive social and economic wreckage.

The ideology of the new Republic seemed to promote significant social changes. Many of the most obvious dealt with slavery and women's rights. These areas of potential change were affected, but not very profoundly. A gradual process of changing the status of slaves in the North began, but was incomplete well into the nineteenth century. Southern slaves reaped even fewer benefits. Women had no immediate gains. Native Americans were in for continued conflicts and hardships regardless of the governmental philosophy of the whites. With victory, the struggle for dominance in America again shifted, and this time the contenders were different groups of Americans.

LEARNING OBJECTIVES

Upon completion of the lesson you should develop and be able to demonstrate an understanding of:

1. The writing, nature, and ratification of the Articles of Confederation.
2. The key military events of the Revolutionary War and the nature of the contending armies.
3. The impact of the Revolution on the American economy.
4. The significance of the Revolution for women, slaves, Indians, and loyalists.

KEY TERMS

Look for these items as you proceed through the lesson assignments. Be able to define them upon completion of this lesson.

People

John Adams

Benedict Arnold

General John Burgoyne

Cherokee Indians

General Charles Cornwallis

Thomas Danforth

Silas Deane

John Dickinson

Benjamin Franklin

Horatio Gates

German Mercenaries (Hessians)

Comte de Grasse

Nathaniel Greene

Admiral Richard Howe

General William Howe

Iroquois Indians

John Jay

Daniel Morgan

Robert Morris

Lord North

Thomas Peters

Vergennes

George Washington

Places

Cowpens

Manhattan Island

Staten Island

Yorktown

Events and Terms

Articles of Confederation

Battles of Trenton and Princeton

Battle of Saratoga

Battle of Yorktown

continental dollar

loyalists

privateering

ratification

Second Continental Congress

Treaty of Paris, 1783

Treaty of Alliance (France)

western land claims

Ideas

abolition of slavery

republicanism

TEXT FOCUS POINTS

The following focus points are designed to help you get the most from the text. Review them, then read the assignment. You may want to write notes to reinforce what you have learned.

Text: Nash et al., *The American People*, Chapter 6, pp. 180-202 (end at "Ferment of Revolutionary Politics").

1. Why did the war shift from New England to New York in 1776? What resulted from this shift?
2. What did Washington learn from his early engagements with the British around New York and Philadelphia? What strategy did he develop?
3. The military operations in the North during the American Revolution are outlined on the map found on page 180. What were Washington's movements from July 1776 to January 1777? What were the movements and results of the three British armies headed toward Saratoga? Where is Valley Forge?
4. How did the Second Continental Congress try to legitimize its activities? What were the results of these efforts? Why did the ratification of the government take so long?
5. Study the map on page 187. Where were each of the original thirteen states located? Which ones had western land claims? Where were those claims?
6. Using the map on page 188, what effect did British Indian allies have on the Revolutionary War in the Western Territories? How did the war affect the native American?
7. What were the characteristics of the southern campaign begun by the British in 1778 at Savannah that ended three years later at Yorktown?
8. How did the Americans negotiate such satisfactory peace terms at Paris?
9. What were the ingredients in the American victory?
10. Where and how was the American Army recruited? What were its problems? What were the causes of casualties?
11. How were civilians affected by the war?
12. How did the war affect loyalists and African-Americans?

READER FOCUS POINTS

Reader: *Perspectives on America, Volume I*, "Triumph at Yorktown," by Rudolph.

1. How had the twelve months before the victory at Yorktown been the darkest hours of the struggle for independence?
2. How did a disparate chain of events from the West Indies to New England converge to bring victory?
3. Why did Cornwallis end up at Yorktown?
4. What threads of a victorious strategy was being drawn together by Washington? How was Clinton tricked by Washington to protect New York? What key role did the Comte de Grasse play?
5. How did the American-French forces achieve victory at Yorktown?

VIDEO FOCUS POINTS

The following focus points are designed to help you get the most from the video segment of this lesson. Review them, then watch the video. You may want to write notes to reinforce what you have learned.

Video: "A Revolution for Independence"

Synopsis: Addresses the nature of the military conflict between England and the United States, and the differences and similarities between the opposing forces.

1. Why did the Americans appear to be overmatched by the regular British Army?
2. What was Professor Peter Maslowski's assessment of the comparative powers?
3. What did Professor Maslowski say was the significance of the Battles of Trenton and Princeton?
4. What happened that led to the American victory at Saratoga?
5. What were the general characteristics of the southern phase of the Revolutionary War? Why were the British finally forced to Yorktown?

---

6. What was Professor Maslowski's analysis of the significance of the Battles at Saratoga and Yorktown? Why did the Americans win the war?

OPTIONAL ACTIVITY

Write a two-page essay on life during The Revolutionary War. Take a role, such as a fighter, politician, housewife, seaport laborer, or farmer. Research the activities and experiences of such people and write a first-person account.

SUGGESTED READINGS

Further readings can be found in the text on page 219. Of special interest is *The Birth of the Republic, 1763-1789* by Edmund S. Morgan; *For the Common Defense,* by Maslowski and Millett.

HISTORICAL PERSPECTIVE

Some authorities argue that the British lost the Revolutionary War more than the Americans won it. Make a list of all the factors which the Americans contributed to victory, such as, tenacity, tactics, morale, and Washington's leadership. Then contrast that with a list of all the apparent shortcomings and mistakes of the British. Which list best explains the victory? How would you integrate such factors as foreign involvement and internal dissension in England? After making these lists, try to write a one-page explanation of the victory of the United States in the War for Independence.

PRACTICE TEST

To help you evaluate your understanding of the lesson, turn to Appendix B and complete the Practice Test for the lesson. The Practice Test contains multiple-choice questions and essay questions, followed by a Feedback Report with correct answers and references.

Lesson 9

The Problems of Confederation

LESSON ASSIGNMENTS

Review the following assignments in order to schedule your time appropriately. Pay careful attention; the titles and numbers of the textbook chapter, the telecourse guide lesson, and the video program may be different from one another.

Text: Nash et al., *The American People, Volume One: To 1877*,
        Chapter 6, "A People in Revolution," pp. 202-219 (begin with
        "Ferment of Revolutionary Politics,") and
        Chapter 7, "Consolidating the Revolution," pp. 220-233 (end at
        "Toward a New National Government.")

Video: "The Problems of Confederation,"
        from the series, *The American Adventure*.

OVERVIEW

The American Republic faced difficult problems such as disputes over navigation of the Ohio and Mississippi Rivers, controversies over banking and commerce in the Northeast, and armed rebelliousness in Springfield, Massachusetts. Considered are the perilous conditions and problems of the United Sates from 1781-1787 and how the state and central governments dealt with them.

INTRODUCTION

Winning independence was only the first step for the United States. To sustain independence and to provide liberty with security were the tasks at hand. The "revolutionary republicanism" of the founders was based on a faith in local government and the good will and honesty of the citizens. The foundation of the country would be the general virtue and reliability of the people. A strong central government was viewed as undesirable and a dangerous bastion of monarchy. To these republicans, the state government should be the main element of political power. State constitutions were framed with care and dedication to principles learned over decades of colonial experience and political theorizing. Legislative branches dominated a weakened executive office. The judicial system reflected the principles of common law rights. Several of the states, following the example George Mason established in Virginia, included specific bills of rights to guarantee the liberties of the citizens. But try as they might, the states could not settle many of the broader, crushing issues facing the Republic, such as the national debt and foreign problems.

The central government established a plan for westward movement. The Land Ordinance of 1785 provided for the dividing of the Northwest Territory into townships and sections and for the selling of the land. The law also promoted education by setting aside one section of land per township to support schools. The Northwest Ordinance of 1787 provided a means of governance which would eventually lead to statehood for the territories created in the Northwest. This was a significant break with past imperial traditions of controlling the territories for the good of the mother country.

The success of the Articles Congress in creating land policies in the Northwest Territory was more than offset by glaring deficiencies. The economic condition of the country was dismal. The states issued currency, the Confederation issued currency, war bonds circulated at a discount, and foreign currencies were common. Except for specie (gold and silver), no American currency was dependable. Besides currency woes, the country faced a staggering war debt. The states and the Confederation governments owed their citizens, soldiers, and foreign lenders millions of dollars. Commercial interests had yet to generate new markets and no central tariff policy existed. In short, the economic affairs of the country were chaotic.

The young country was also beset by severe foreign obstacles. England irritated the states by refusing to remove its troops from forts (trading posts) in the Northwest Territory. England continued to trade firearms with native Americans. It seemed that English officials expected the United States to fall apart. As if the English in Canada did not provide enough friction, the Spanish on the southern border were hostile. The Spanish declared the Mississippi River and the port at New Orleans closed to American trade, and they pushed the Florida boundary nearly two hundred miles to the north. A negotiated settlement by John Jay with Don Diego de

Gardoqui of Spain was unsuccessful. The country was perilously perched between two foes, each attempting to undermine the country's future.

The states also bristled with dissension from within. Debtor-creditor strife broke out in several forms. In Rhode Island, the debtors passed a law making war bonds legal tender. Creditors protested loudly and even ran from their debtors to avoid being paid. Officials in other states feared similar actions in their areas. But the most prominent conflict erupted in Massachusetts. Disgruntled farmers who were unable to pay their mortgages attempted to *stop* foreclosures by preventing the county courts from holding their sessions. At Springfield, Massachusetts, in January 1787 a brief battle occurred between protesters led by Daniel Shays and troops protecting the Federal arsenal. Although of little military significance, the incident was a catalyst for those seeking to alter the nature of the Articles' government. Shays's Rebellion had importance far beyond its limited scope. The country again confronted the problems of providing security while maintaining liberty.

LEARNING OBJECTIVES

Upon completion of the lesson you should develop and be able to demonstrate an understanding of:

1. The relationship between revolutionary republicanism and the political ideas embedded in the state constitutions written between 1775 and 1781.
2. The critical issues of the Confederation period, including what to do about wartime loyalists, Church-state relations, and economic policies.
3. The laws passed by the Confederation Congresses to deal with questions of settling and administering western lands.
4. The critical difficulties the Confederation Congresses had with commercial, financial, and foreign policies.
5. The causes and results of Shays's Rebellion.

KEY TERMS

Look for these items as you proceed through the lesson assignments. Be able to define them upon completion of this lesson.

People

Abigail Adams
John Adams
Jonathan Boucher
Don Diego de Gardoqui
Iroquois Indians

John Jay
Esther DeBerdt Reed
Daniel Shays
George Washington

Places

Fort Detroit
Fort Michilimackinac
Fort Niagara
Mississippi River

New Orleans
Northwest Territory
Ohio River

Events and Terms

Bill for Establishing Religious Freedom
Land Ordinance, 1785
Loyalists
Massachusetts State Constitution
Northwest Ordinance, 1787
paper money
Patriots of '76

Pennsylvania State Constitution
popular politics
provisional congress
revolutionary republicanism
section
Shays's Rebellion
township

Ideas

equality
factions
separation of church and state

new identity
republic
liberty vs. Power

TEXT FOCUS POINTS

The following focus points are designed to help you get the most from the text. Review them, then read the assignment. You may want to write notes to reinforce what you have learned.

Text: Nash et al., *The American People*, Chapter 6, pp. 202-219 (begin with "Ferment of Revolutionary Politics"); and Chapter 7, pp. 220-233 (end at "Toward a New National Government").

1. How did the press, pulpit, and extra-legal committees help to get the revolutionary message across to the people?
2. How did the people's political behavior and ideas change during the revolutionary period?
3. How did the Republican ideology help to define the United States as a free and separate nation?
4. What methods, ideals, and goals characterized the writing of the constitutions in the states? What does the chart on page 208 indicate about the composition of the various state assemblies? What were some limits of citizenship?
5. How did the new governments within the states deal with questions of church-state, loyalists, and slavery?
6. How well did revolutionary politics handle economic problems?
7. How did demobilizing the army present the Confederation government some serious problems?
8. What specific laws and policies were established to deal with western land questions?
9. By studying the map and diagram on page 224, answer these questions:
   A. Where is the Northwest Territory? What modern states were formed from this land?
   B. What is a township? How was it divided? What was the sixteenth section set aside to support?
10. What financial difficulties faced the Confederation in the 1780s?
11. According to the map on page 226, what were the locations of Spanish, British, and United States territory in 1783? What foreign problems had yet to be resolved?

---

12. What was Shays's Rebellion? What impact did it have on the Federalists?

VIDEO FOCUS POINTS

The following focus points are designed to help you get the most from the video segment of this lesson. Review them, then watch the video. You may want to write notes to reinforce what you have learned.

Video: "The Problems of Confederation."

Synopsis: Addresses the problems of maintaining liberty and security for all the people while being confronted by economic, political , and internal dissension.

1. What were the critical ideals holding the country together?
2. What were the critical problems pulling the country apart? Why were the state governments poorly equipped to deal with them?
3. What issues did Professor Forrest McDonald suggest were the most difficult for the state governments to handle?
4. What foreign hostilities confronted the United States in the 1780s? With what results?
5. According to Professor McDonald, what were the primary reasons for a move toward a stronger central government in 1786-87?

OPTIONAL LEARNING ACTIVITIES

1. Read the analysis of Indian treaties on pages 228-229 in the textbook. In a two-page paper, write a reaction to the relationship between the treaties and realities of ultimate settlements.
2. The Articles of Confederation had some obvious defects. Write a two-page proposal for changes that could allow the government to effectively operate without removing the *primary* authority from the states. With these changes, what kind of a government would the United States have?

SUGGESTED READINGS

Further readings can be found in the text on pages 219, and 243. Of particular interest is *E Pluribus Unum by* Forrest McDonald.

HISTORICAL PERSPECTIVE

The transition from revolution to a stable government is always difficult. Establishing authority and implementing radical ideals are complicated tasks. The United States had the especially hard time of balancing liberty and authority. The variety of state governments established is a good indicator of the many divergent opinions of the time. What were the most difficult issues to resolve on the local level? On the central level? How do those problems compare to modern revolutionary experiences in the world? What elements of these modern experiences are most like those of the eighteenth century United States? Most dissimilar?

PRACTICE TEST

To help you evaluate your understanding of the lesson, turn to Appendix B and complete the Practice Test for the lesson. The Practice Test contains multiple-choice questions and essay questions, followed by a Feedback Report with correct answers and references.

Lesson 10

Creating a Stronger Union

LESSON ASSIGNMENTS

Review the following assignments in order to schedule your time appropriately. Pay careful attention; the titles and numbers of the textbook chapter, the telecourse guide lesson, and the video program may be different from one another.

Text: Nash et al., *The American People, Volume One: To 1877*, Chapter 7, "Consolidating the Revolution," pp. 233-243; and Chapter 8, "Creating a Nation," pp. 244-255.

Reader: *Perspectives on America, Volume I*, "Business of the Highest Magnitude," by Alberts.

Video: "Creating a Stronger Union," from the series, *The American Adventure*.

OVERVIEW

Independence Hall in Philadelphia was the scene of another step in the evolvement of a firmer union, and statehouses like the one in Hartford, Connecticut were places where the fate of the Constitution was decided. This program describes how centralists won the struggle for a stronger government and traces the origin, writing, ratification, and implementation of the United States Constitution.

INTRODUCTION

While many capable and influential American citizens were aware of the difficulties of the Confederation government, most of the people did not realize the serious problems facing the country.

The Potomac Conference of 1785 and the Annapolis Conference of 1786 considered serious commercial questions from a regional perspective, but they failed to answer the larger concerns about power, political equality, and the role of central government. Alexander Hamilton and James Madison asked their home states to call for a comprehensive reform of the government. The calls of Virginia and the Confederation Congress for a national convention to amend the Articles were eventually heeded by twelve of the states in 1787.

The delegates who assembled in Philadelphia in the spring and summer of 1787 decided to propose a totally different government than the one called for in the Articles. The tense and frequently heated debates during the convention produced a document that provided for a much stronger central government while protecting many of the vested interests of the various regions and states. The agreed-to government was to have a structure similar to the governments of the various states. It would have control over commerce, currency, defense, and justice.

The proposition of a stronger central government was one thing, but its acceptance and implementation were something else altogether. The delegates decided that ratification should be by special convention in each state, and a favorable vote in nine of the conventions would start the new government. The proponents, calling themselves Federalists, argued that a change was necessary to avoid national catastrophe and that the Constitution was the best alternative available. The opponents, or Anti-Federalists, objected, among other things, to the lack of a Bill of Rights, the weakening of the states' autonomy and the unrestricted re-election of a president.

Despite several close calls, the Federalists prevailed in eleven conventions by the end of July 1788. In its last official act, the Articles' Congress called for the election of the House of Representatives, the appointment of Senators and the selection of presidential electors. They adjourned for the last time when the new Congress assembled.

On April 30, 1789, President Washington accepted the oath of office and the new government slowly moved into action. The Congress initiated several significant pieces of legislation. In separate bills, Congress created the executive departments including State, Treasury, and War, each with its own secretary. In later years, these department heads became known as the president's Cabinet. The Judiciary Act of 1789 established a federal court system with thirteen district courts, three circuit courts of appeals, and a Supreme Court composed of a chief justice and five associates. The act defined a broad spectrum of federal jurisdiction and provided the president with an attorney general. The first Congress also passed a series of amendments to the Constitution to ensure basic rights to individuals. Ten of these were accepted by the required three-fourths of the states and became known as the Bill of Rights. (Note: Two hundred years later, the eleventh of these twelve was ratified as the twenty-seventh amendment.)

The domestic policies of the Washington administration were dominated by Secretary of the Treasury Alexander Hamilton. Hamilton, unlike the revolutionary radical republicans, believed that the people were generally motivated by self-interests and that the common masses were very untrustworthy. Therefore, he created a financial system for the new government designed to ensure the support of the rich and well-born. These policies caused rigorous debate and helped create an opposition political faction headed by James Madison, and Secretary of State, Thomas Jefferson. The dream of the Federalists for a stronger central government was realized, but its ability to survive both internal and external threats was still uncertain.

LEARNING OBJECTIVES

Upon completion of the lesson you should develop and be able to demonstrate an understanding of:

1. The series of attempts to revise the Articles of Confederation and the eventual assembly of the Constitutional Convention.
2. The nature of the Constitutional Convention including:
    A. the roles of the various delegates.
    B. the debates over various plans and proposals.
    C. the compromises that allowed the completion of the document.
3. The ratification of the Constitution including:
    A. method.
    B. debates between supporters and opponents.
    C. the reasons for its acceptance.
4. The organization of the government during Washington's administration.
5. The philosophies of Hamilton and Jefferson, and the debates over Hamilton's financial policies and proposals.

KEY TERMS

Look for these items as you proceed through the lesson assignments. Be able to define them upon completion of this lesson.

People

Benjamin Franklin
Alexander Hamilton
Patrick Henry
John Jay
James Madison

George Mason
William Paterson
John Rutledge
Roger Sherman
George Washington

Places

Federal Hall, New York City
Independence Hall

Philadelphia

Events and Terms

Annapolis Convention
Anti-Federalists
Assumption
Convention
Bank of the United States
ratification
Report of Public Credit
Secretary of Treasury
Virginia Plan
Whiskey Rebellion

Great Compromise
New Jersey Plan
Philadelphia (Constitutional)

Bill of Rights
3/5ths Compromise
electoral college
Federalists
Funding

Idea

checks and balances

TEXT FOCUS POINTS

The following focus points are designed to help you get the most from the text. Review them, then read the assignment. You may want to write notes to reinforce what you have learned.

Text: Nash et al., *The American People*, Chapter 7, pp. 233-243; and Chapter 8, pp. 244-255.

1. Who were the Federalists? Why did they believe the nation was in political crisis in the 1780s?
2. What previous convention led to the Constitutional (Philadelphia) Convention? What were the delegates to Philadelphia authorized to do?
3. Who were the leading delegates to the convention? What roles did they play?
4. What were the Virginia and New Jersey Plans? What were their crucial differences? What was the Great Compromise?
5. What were the other major issues and compromises which were finally made part of the Constitution?
6. What were the major arguments of the Federalists and Anti-Federalists over ratification of the Constitution? How were their visions different?
7. Using the map on page 241, where were the major areas of Federalist and Anti-Federalist support concentrated?
8. What was the outcome of the various state ratifying conventions? What was the "social geography" of ratification?
9. Who was chosen to lead the new government?
10. How did the Bill of Rights become part of the Constitution?
11. What were Hamilton's basic political views? What were the elements of his economic plans? What people disagreed with his plans and philosophy? With what results?

READER FOCUS POINTS

Reader: *Perspectives on America, Volume I*, "Business of the Highest Magnitude,"
   by Alberts.

1. What were the Pennsylvania Democrats major objections to the new Constitution?
2. What maneuvers did the Pennsylvania Federalists make to get a convention called? How did the Democrats try to keep the ratifying convention from meeting? How did the Federalists get a quorum present in order to complete the establishment of time and place for the ratifying convention to meet?
3. How did the Pennsylvania ratification convention decide the issue?

VIDEO FOCUS POINTS

The following focus points are designed to help you get the most from the video segment of this lesson. Review them, then watch the video. You may want to write notes to reinforce what you have learned.

Video: "Creating a Stronger Union"

Synopsis: Addresses the interplay of ideals, personalities, and needs that led to the writing and reatification of the United States Consitution.

1. What forces were leading to revision of the government?
2. Why did the delegates keep their debates secret?
3. What was the debate over representation? What compromise resulted?
4. How was the issue of slavery reflected in the debates? With what results?
5. How did the delegates ensure that the "right" kind of people would run the government?
6. According to Professor Forrest McDonald, why did the delegates eventually agree to the Constitution? Why did the Constitution succeed?
7. Why were some people outraged at what the delegates had done? According to Professor McDonald, what were the most valid objections to the Constitution?

8. What role did the Federalist Papers play in ratification?
9. What was Washington's trip to New York City like?

OPTIONAL LEARNING ACTIVITY

In a two-page essay, compare and contrast the nature and significance of the Stamp Act riot in Boston (1765—Lesson 7), Shays's Rebellion (Lesson 9), and the Whiskey Rebellion. Analyze the differences in dealing with the disturbances and their impacts. What do these differences reveal about the new federal government?

SUGGESTED READINGS

Further readings can be found in the text on pages 243 and 268-269. Of special interest is *Novus Ordo Seclorum* by Forrest McDonald.

HISTORICAL PERSPECTIVE

The Federalists wanted a stronger central government. In what significant ways was the United States government more powerful under the Constitution? The supporters of the Constitution were also the implementers of the new government. How did their actions (especially legislation and executive policy recommendations) reveal an even stronger commitment to central authority than the document itself might imply? To what degree did these Federalists believe in states' rights?

PRACTICE TEST

To help you evaluate your understanding of the lesson, turn to Appendix B and complete the Practice Test for the lesson. The Practice Test contains multiple-choice questions and essay questions, followed by a Feedback Report with correct answers and references.

Lesson 11

The Republic in a Hostile World

LESSON ASSIGNMENTS

Review the following assignments in order to schedule your time appropriately. Pay careful attention; the titles and numbers of the textbook chapter, the telecourse guide lesson, and the video program may be different from one another.

Text: Nash et al., *The American People, Volume One: To 1877*, Chapter 8, "Creating a Nation," pp. 255-268.

Reader   *Perspectives on America, Volume I*, "Liberté, Egalité, Anemosité," by Wills.

Video: "The Republic in a Hostile World," from the series, *The American Adventure*.

OVERVIEW

The continued occupation of forts like Niagara, agitation in the newspapers, and protests to Federalists' policies threatened the survival of the United States in the 1790s. Described are the critical foreign affairs problems the United States faced during the Federalist period and how the Republic's leadership got the nation through these storms.

INTRODUCTION

The United States faced a hostile and violent Atlantic world in the 1790s. Although England and Spain had been hostile since the end of the Revolutionary War, the foreign problems of the 1790s revolved around a general European war that followed the outbreak of the French Revolution. The American political reaction to the war in Europe became so disruptive that the security of the United States was threatened.

The British had been unwilling to remove troops from American soil as required by the Treaty of Paris of 1783. England was a reluctant trade partner as well. But these problems could have been solved with time and effort. The war generated by the French Revolution posed a greater threat to the United States. When the European monarchies joined forces to stamp out the revolutionary "terror," the United States became a pawn in the ever-widening conflict. Just as significantly, American public opinion was sharply divided between pro-French and pro-British sentiments.

Both France and England wanted and needed American commerce. Each also wanted to stop the other from receiving American goods. The simple dictum of "neutral ships made neutral goods" was unsatisfactory to each. Thus, American commercial vessels were subject to seizure by both powers. The British went even further by claiming the right to "impress" any "British citizen" into the royal navy even if they were on board a neutral ship. The English captains frequently impressed Americans, which infuriated the United States. But, before any effective solution to the English policies could be devised, the actions of French Ambassador Edmund Genêt overshadowed these problems. Genêt violated American neutrality when he attempted to recruit privateers and soldiers to fight the English and Spanish. Genêt's activities embarrassed the Washington administration and divided American public opinion even further. Genêt was finally told to leave the United States.

Genêt's dismissal ended the immediate tensions with France in 1794. The British question was then confronted. Chief Justice John Jay was sent to England to negotiate a settlement with the British. Jay's Treaty was very unpopular in the United States. It was given only faint praise even by the Federalists. But the treaty was much better than the apparent alternative of war with England. Besides avoiding a war, Jay's Treaty had another benefit. It persuaded the Spanish to settle their differences with the United States. The resulting agreement, called Pinckney's Treaty, opened the Mississippi River and New Orleans to American trade and reestablished the 31st parallel as Florida's northern boundary with the United States.

The deep political divisions within the country over these foreign policies convinced Washington to retire after two terms in office. He was sensitive to the strongly worded, partisan attacks of the Jeffersonian-Republican Press. In the Election of 1796, the Federalist candidate John Adams narrowly defeated Thomas Jefferson for president. The electoral vote split in such a way that Thomas Jefferson got the second largest number of electoral votes and became vice president. The long-term friendship between the two shattered early in the presidency of John Adams and for nearly two decades they remained bitter political foes.

The presidency of John Adams was dominated by foreign affairs. The French were very upset by both the Jay Treaty and the election results. A diplomatic blunder, called the XYZ Affair, led to an undeclared war between the two countries from 1798-1800. The Federalists in Congress used the war hysteria as an excuse to try to eliminate their Republican opposition. They passed a series of acts to try to stifle dissent. The measures, known as the Alien and Sedition Acts, were put to vicious use. Several outspoken Republicans were arrested, tried, imprisoned, and fined. Thomas Jefferson and James Madison led protests in the form of the Kentucky and Virginia Resolutions, respectively. The escalating confrontation was defused by the Convention of 1800, a negotiated settlement between the United States and France. The Alien and Sedition Acts were no longer necessary and could no longer be used to control Republicans. Many of the Federalist leaders were disgruntled with the president for avoiding a war which might have allowed them to vanquish both their foreign and domestic foes.

The Federalist leaders might have been unhappy, but the general citizenry was delighted. President Adams ran for reelection in 1800. The Republicans again ran Thomas Jefferson and Aaron Burr. The electoral college vote was again confusing. John Adams got 65 votes and Charles Cotesworth Pinckney got 64; but Thomas Jefferson and Aaron Burr each received 73 votes. Technically, no one had a majority, so the decision went to the House of Representatives where each state delegation was to have one vote to break the deadlock. Unhappy Federalists made one last, desperate effort to deny their chief antagonist the presidency by supporting Aaron Burr. Finally, after thirty-five ballots, the impasse was broken and Jefferson was elected on the thirty-sixth vote of the House, ten states to four, and two abstentions. The Federalists had lost control of the presidency for the first time, never to recapture it. The tumult of war and political divisiveness had brought the Jeffersonians triumphantly to power.

LEARNING OBJECTIVES

Upon completion of the lesson you should develop and be able to demonstrate an understanding of:

1. The complex foreign problems confronted by the United States during Washington's administrations.
2. The political and social tensions of the United States in the 1790s.
3. The problems between the United States and France during the presidency of John Adams.
4. The intentions and results of the Alien and Sedition Acts.
5. The accomplishments and failures of the Federalists.

KEY TERMS

Look for these items as you proceed through the lesson assignments. Be able to define them upon completion of this lesson.

People

John Adams	John Jay
Luther Baldwin	Thomas Jefferson
Aaron Burr	Louis XVI
James Callender	Timothy Pickering
Edmund Genêt	Talleyrand
Alexander Hamilton	

Places

Charleston, South Carolina	Prussia

Events and Terms

Alien and Sedition Acts	Kentucky Resolution
Democratic-Republican Societies	Pinckney Treaty
French Alliance, 1778	Virginia Resolution

Continued on next page

French Revolution   XYZ Affair
Jay's Treaty, 1795

Idea

nullification

TEXT FOCUS POINTS

The following focus points are designed to help you get the most from the text. Review them, then read the assignment. You may want to write notes to reinforce what you have learned.

Text: Nash et al., *The American People*, Chapter 8, pp. 255-268.

1. Why and how had the French Revolution become a threat to American security?
2. Who was Edmund Genêt and how did he intensify the divisions between Federalists and Republicans over foreign policy?
3. What were the reasons for Jay's Treaty and why was it so controversial?
4. What was significant about the political mood in 1796? Who won the presidential election of that year?
5. What brought about a crisis with France during the administration of John Adams?
6. What were the Alien and Sedition Acts? Why were they passed? With what results?
7. What formal opposition was there to the Alien and Sedition measures?
8. What was unusual about the election of 1800? Who won?
9. According to the map on page 265, where were the major areas that supported John Adams? Which areas supported Thomas Jefferson?
10. What were the differences between Republicans and Federalists?

READER FOCUS POINTS

Reader: *Perspectives on America, Volume I*, "Liberté, Egalité, Anemosité," by Wills.

1. What lead to mutual misapprehension between Americans and Frenchmen over the French revolution?
2. How did Jefferson and Hamilton disagree over the French Revolution and the Treaty of Alliance with France after the revolution broke out?
3. How did the news of Louis XVI execution affect American politics? How did Edmond Genêt further dissension in the United States? What finally happened to Genêt?
4. How did the Democratic-Republican Societies further divide the country?
5. How did Jefferson appraise the French Revolution in his later years?

VIDEO FOCUS POINTS

The following focus points are designed to help you get the most from the video segment of this lesson. Review them, then watch the video. You may want to write notes to reinforce what you have learned.

Video: "The Republic in a Hostile World"

Synopsis: Addresses the critical problems that the United States faced in foreign affairs during the Federalist Period and how these problems influenced American political and social development.

1. How did American public opinion divide over sympathy with the French or British?
2. What did Edmund Genêt do to alienate the Washington administration?
3. What are the key differences between Jeffersonian and Hamiltonian ideas?
4. Who was James Callender? What did he do? With what result?
5. Why did Jefferson write the Kentucky Resolution? Why anonymously?
6. According to Professor McDonald, why were foreign countries so hostile to the United States? Why did the Federalists risk the Alien and Sedition Acts?

OPTIONAL LEARNING ACTIVITY

Read the text and examine the picture of George Washington on pages 250-251. Discuss in a two-page paper what the different images reveal about Washington's status. How had attitudes toward him obviously changed during his years of leadership? How might an earlier portrait of Washington exhibit other characteristics?

SUGGESTED READINGS

Further readings can be found in the text on page 268-269. Of special interest is *The Presidency of George Washington* by Forrest McDonald.

HISTORICAL PERSPECTIVE

The Federalists accomplished a great deal during the twelve years they controlled the central government. Among their more significant contributions were: the creation of a national currency, the establishment of a national bank, the maintenance of peace, the negotiation of a treaty with the Native Americans in the Ohio Valley, and the entrenchment of a stronger national government. Despite these accomplishments, the Federalists lost political power and eventually disappeared from the scene. What weaknesses in the Federalists' political attitudes made such an end seemingly inevitable? What could they have done to remain a viable political force?

PRACTICE TEST

To help you evaluate your understanding of the lesson, turn to Appendix B and complete the Practice Test for the lesson. The Practice Test contains multiple-choice questions and essay questions, followed by a Feedback Report with correct answers and references.

Lesson 12

The Rural Republic

LESSON ASSIGNMENTS

Review the following assignments in order to schedule your time appropriately. Pay careful attention; the titles and numbers of the textbook chapter, the telecourse guide lesson, and the video program may be different from one another.

Text: Nash et al., *The American People, Volume One: To 1877*,
         Chapter 9, "Society and Politics in the Early Republic," pp. 276-289 and pp. 295-305.

Video: "The Rural Republic,"
         from the series, *The American Adventure*.

OVERVIEW

A social portrait is drawn of the values and attitudes of rural America as it hovered on the brink of transformation by industrial, urban and population forces. The hard but unhurried life of trans-Appalachian pioneers is told from the Rural Life Museum in Norris, Tennessee.

INTRODUCTION

The United States was a rural republic as the nineteenth century began. The ancient cycles of planting and harvesting still prevailed throughout the country. The ever-advancing frontier was a product of this rural heritage. The characteristics, attitudes, and beliefs of rural inhabitants formed an essential element of American ideology and mythology. But change was on the horizon. During the first half of the century, the United States would begin to feel the transforming power of the industrial fires. The independent, self-sufficient individual was replaced by the interdependent city dweller. The dominance of the rural lifestyle began to melt away. A glimpse of that rural heritage helps explain the ambivalence of America's present ideology.

Rural America in 1800 was well typified by the life led by the settlers just west of the Appalachian Mountains. Their homesteads began with the lonely, solemn sound of an axe on virgin timber. Their initial survival depended upon the ability to clear the land, build shelter, and acquire food. The first years were monotonous, lonely, and hard. But for many, the exhilaration of pioneering was the most notable experience of their lives.

The isolated homesteaders were soon joined by others seeking land and pursuing a dream. As the population concentrated in some areas, communities evolved. Stabilizing institutions such as schools, churches, and town governments developed bringing social conformity and legal order. The settlers made the most of every opportunity to congregate. The community center was frequently the church, which often doubled as the meeting hall and schoolhouse.

The rural inhabitants took pride in their hospitality and self-sufficiency. The settlers believed in the equality of men, and that the best would succeed if given an opportunity. They had little use for the idle, whether they were rich or poor.

The society had clearly defined roles for the members of the community. Women were tied to the home as wife and mother. Their responsibilities were great and life for them was hard. Children had little free time. Generally, female children helped in the home and male children worked in the fields. The opportunity for schooling was usually very limited for boys, almost non-existent for girls. Minority populations lived on the fringe of the community and were usually discriminated against.

Close-knit, agricultural communities still dominated the United States in 1800. But within the next half-century, dominance shifted to the cities, with their urban concerns and attitudes. The rural roots of modern America soon became a distant memory.

LEARNING OBJECTIVES

Upon completion of the lesson you should develop and be able to demonstrate an understanding of:

1. The character and nature of rural society at the beginning of the nineteenth century.
2. The social and political ideas which emerged from this society.
3. The various social roles of women, children, and minorities.

KEY TERMS

Look for these items as you proceed through the lesson assignments. Be able to define them upon completion of this lesson.

People

Thomas Malthus   Gabriel Prosser
Judith Sargeant Murray   Eli Whitney

Places

Haiti   Richmond, Virginia
Norris, Tennessee   South
Northeast   West

Events and Terms

National Road   divorce
"free blacks"

Ideas

equal opportunity   poverty
individualism   social equality

TEXT FOCUS POINTS

The following focus points are designed to help you get the most from the text. Review them, then read the assignment. You may want to write notes to reinforce what you have learned.

Text: Nash et al., *The American People*, Chapter 9, pp. 276-289 and 295-305.

1. What were the primary elements of the Jeffersonian Vision? How could the vision be best protected from the corrupting influences of urban concentrations of wealth?
2. What were the regional differences between the Northeast and South in economic and social terms?
3. What were the characteristics of trans-Appalachian life? Why were local communities so important?
4. What were the patterns of wealth and poverty in early nineteenth century America? What attempts were made to alleviate poverty?
5. What characterized the lives of women and blacks in this period?

VIDEO FOCUS POINTS

The following focus points are designed to help you get the most from the video segment of this lesson. Review them, then watch the video. You may want to write notes to reinforce what you have learned.

Video: "The Rural Republic"

Synopsis: Addresses the character of rural life in America about 1800.

1. What were the initial priorities for establishing a homestead?
2. What were the routines of a pioneer family?
3. What did Professor Julie Jeffrey say were the reasons for success or failure?
4. What elements of community were initially created by the settlers?
5. What beliefs and ideas did Professor Jeffrey suggest came from these settlement experiences?

OPTIONAL LEARNING ACTIVITY

Life in preindustrial America was significantly different than everyday life in 1850. In a two-page essay, compare and contrast the changes in timeliness, isolation, institutions, and trade between urban and rural living. How had these changes transformed even agricultural regions?

SUGGESTED READINGS

Further readings can be found in the text on pages 316-317.

HISTORICAL PERSPECTIVE

Rural values and social structures deeply influenced important Americans like Thomas Jefferson. How did these attitudes vary from the commercial and urban values of the Northeast? Which rural values remained vital in American thought, despite the changes in rural society? Which attitudes virtually disappeared? Do you think these rural values formed an appropriate base for modern, urban America values? Why or why not?

PRACTICE TEST

To help you evaluate your understanding of the lesson, turn to Appendix B and complete the Practice Test for the lesson. The Practice Test contains multiple-choice questions and essay questions, followed by a Feedback Report with correct answers and references.

Lesson 13

The Failure of Diplomacy

LESSON ASSIGNMENTS

Review the following assignments in order to schedule your time appropriately. Pay careful attention; the titles and numbers of the textbook chapter, the telecourse guide lesson, and the video program may be different from one another.

Text: Nash et al., *The American People, Volume One: To 1877*, Chapter 9, "Society and Politics in the Early Republic," pp. 271-280 and pp. 305-309 (to "The United States and the Americas").

Video: "The Failure of Diplomacy," from the series, *The American Adventure*.

Reader: *Perspectives on America, Volume I,* "Timid President? Futile War?," by Brant.

OVERVIEW

Confrontations along the Great Lakes, at Washington, D.C., and New Orleans, illustrate the failure of diplomacy in avoiding a war nobody wanted. Explored are the Jeffersonian Republicans' responses to power, and the foreign problems which impinged upon them to the end of the War of 1812. The significance of the War of 1812 is analyzed.

INTRODUCTION

The Jeffersonian-Republicans faced a new challenge in 1801—how to lead the government. After years of opposing the Federalists, Thomas Jefferson had won the election prize. With power came different responsibilities. Jefferson immediately established a new tone for the government, now located in the half-completed, partly-occupied Federal District of Columbia. He created a "democratic" style of government that was less formal during both public and private occasions.

Jefferson's decisions with regard to previous Federalist policies were pragmatic. The most odious of their policies, the Alien and Sedition Acts and the Whiskey Tax, were allowed to expire. But the core of Hamilton's financial policies of funding, assumption, and the national bank were continued and, in some cases, even improved. In one area, however, the Republicans struck with a vengeance—the federal judiciary. The Republican Congress repealed the Judiciary Act of 1801, thus unseating the newly appointed district and circuit judges. The justices of the peace appointed for Washington, D.C., were left alone, except for those who had not received their papers of appointment. This situation led to the *Marbury v. Madison* Supreme Court decision. Jefferson also supported impeachment as a means of remodeling the bench, a tactic that was dropped when the impeachment of Samuel Chase, associate justice of the Supreme Court, failed.

Despite these internal political concerns, the first two Republican presidencies were most seriously challenged by renewed conflict in Europe. The Continent's temporary peace was shattered in 1803 by the eruption of the Napoleonic Wars. At first the war actually benefitted the United States. Napoleon, realizing the vulnerability of New World colonies, sold the Louisiana Territory to the United States. Although France's ownership of the territory was dubious, and the power of the Constitutional government to make such a deal debatable, Jefferson seized Napoleon's offer to purchase half of the Mississippi Valley for $15 million. But by 1806, the deadlocked struggle between England and France threatened American interests.

The United States was the most important single carrier of overseas goods. With the military powers stalemated, the belligerents turned to economic coercion. For each, this meant stopping American trade with the enemy. Neither made any concessions to neutral rights. Initially, the United States resisted British and French actions equally. A series of Congressional actions failed to ease the problems.

By 1811 several factors focused American hostilities on England. First, in 1811, the northern Ohio Valley erupted into Indian war. The Tecumseh Rebellion was actually the result of the natives' anger over the movement of whites into the area. But Americans accused the British of instigating the uprising. The Westerners wanted to remove English influence from all of North America. Second, English-American relations were damaged by diplomatic foul-ups. An apparent agreement between the English ambassador and the Secretary of State was summarily dismissed by the British Foreign Office and the ambassador recalled and replaced. The next two representatives of the crown contributed further to the deteriorating relations. The third factor was the increasing influence of a group of young nationalistic Republican politicians called the "War Hawks."

Jefferson had retired from office in 1809, replaced by his friend and fellow Virginian, James Madison. Madison did not want war. But by 1812, he could not tolerate further English offenses. In June of that year, he reluctantly asked for war. By the end of the month hostilities were declared. Thus began a war neither side wanted, but which each refused to avoid.

The War of 1812 was a seemingly futile and fruitless conflict. The declaration of war came a couple of days after the English Prime Minister had promised to repeal restrictions (Orders in Council) against American shipping. The major campaigns by both antagonists were largely failures. The most significant British assault was the capture of Washington, D.C., where they burned many official buildings and then abandoned the city. The most astonishing American victory came at New Orleans where Andrew Jackson repelled a British attack, inflicting incredible losses on the Redcoats. However, the victory came a few weeks after peace was agreed to in Europe. As if these were not ironies enough, in the aftermath of this insignificant conflict, the United States developed a new political consensus, economic status, and nationalistic frenzy. The Republicans had led the Republic through a second decade of European conflict, and into a new era of European peace and American prosperity.

LEARNING OBJECTIVES

Upon completion of this lesson you should develop and be able to demonstrate an understanding of:

1. The "Revolution of 1800" and the changes brought by the Republican control of the government.
2. The foreign problems confronting the United States to 1815 and their impact on the country, including:
    A. the events leading to the acquisition of Louisiana.
    B. the French and English restrictions on the United States and the results on American trade and sailors.
    C. the factors leading to the War of 1812.
    D. the fighting and consequences of the War of 1812 for the United States.

KEY TERMS

Look for these items as you proceed through the lesson assignments. Be able to define them upon completion of this lesson.

People

Aaron Burr
Samuel Chase
William Clark
Andrew Jackson
Thomas Jefferson
Pierre L'Enfant
Meriwether Clark
James Madison

John Marshall
James Monroe
John Pickering
Zebulon Pike
the Prophet
Sacajawea
Talleyrand
Tecumseh

Places

Florida
Louisiana Territory
National Road

Washington, D.C.
West Florida

Events and Terms

Adams-Onis Treaty
Chesapeake-Leopard Affair
Embargo Act, 1807
Hartford Convention
impeachment
impressment
Judiciary Act, 1801
Judiciary Act, 1802

Land Act, 1801
Land Act, 1820
Macon Bill #2
Marbury v. Madison
McCulloch v. Maryland
Non-Intercourse Act
War Hawks

Ideas

judicial review

neutral rights

TEXT FOCUS POINTS

The following focus points are designed to help you get the most from the text. Review them, then read the assignment. You may want to write notes to reinforce what you have learned.

Text: Nash et al., *The American People*, Chapter 9, pp. 271-280 and 305-309 (to "The United States and the Americas").

1. What was the new capital like at Jefferson's inauguration?
2. What were the significances of the inauguration of Jefferson?
3. How and why did the Republicans plan to cleanse the government? With what results for the judicial system?
4. What is the significance of the *Marbury v. Madison* case? *McCulloch v. Maryland?*
5. How did Jefferson dismantle the Federalist war program?
6. Using the map on page 281, how did the Louisiana Purchase come about? With what results? What other territory was acquired? How? What did the explorers of the Louisiana Lands discover?
7. What were Jefferson's principles for foreign affairs and commerce? Why was there a threat to American neutral rights?
8. What policy of coercion did Jefferson attempt? What was the Chesapeake-Leopard incident? What was America's response to it?
9. Who were the War Hawks? What was their position on English violations of neutral rights?
10. How did ineffective American foreign policy and vigorous anti-British efforts of the War Hawks lead to the War of 1812?
11. What were the major military events of the War of 1812? How did New England Federalists react? How and why did the war come to an end?
12. What were the results of the end of the War?
13. What major new initiatives in American foreign policy occurred after the War of 1812 to 1825?

READER FOCUS POINTS

Reader: *Perspectives on America, Volume I,* "Timid President? Futile War? ," by Brant.

1. What picture has been built up over the years of James Madison's role in the War of 1812?
2. What evidence does Brant use to indicate that Madison was in charge, but still a believer in American liberty?
3. What preparations did Madison advise for a land war? What stories were told to imply Madison was incompetent as the war began? How does Brant explain them?
4. Why was Hull's appointment a major, but unforeseeable, blunder? How did Madison react to the disaster?
5. What problems did Madison face with army leadership? What was his role in the burning of Washington, D.C.?
6. What is the author's final analysis of Madison's accomplishments?

VIDEO FOCUS POINTS

The following focus points are designed to help you get the most from the video segment of this lesson. Review them, then watch the video. You may want to write notes to reinforce what you have learned.

Video: "Failure of Diplomacy"

Synopsis: Addresses the impact on the United States of the long and vicious Napoleonic Wars.

1. What factors were involved in the acquisition of Louisiana by the United States?
2. Why and how did France and England violate the neutrality of the United States?
3. How did the United States react to these foreign threats?

4. Why did the United States declare war on England, according to Professor Peter Maslowski?
5. What were the outcomes of the War of 1812?
6. How did Professor Maslowski explain the American sense of victory following the War of 1812?

OPTIONAL LEARNING ACTIVITY

Thomas Jefferson came into the presidency with intentions of limiting the size and power of the central government. In a two-page essay, analyze his successes and failures in accomplishing this goal.

SUGGESTED READINGS

Further readings can be found in the text on page 316-317.

HISTORICAL PERSPECTIVE

The American people were dramatically affected by events in Europe from 1700 to 1815. The colonial wars had, in many ways, prepared the way for independence. Once independent, the United States was buffeted by wars and by the military/commercial policies of Europe. At the conclusion of the War of 1812, however, the Republic no longer greatly suffered from foreign intervention. In fact, the United States actually benefitted from the distress of the European states. What caused this turnabout? Why was the United States able to function more effectively and freely in world affairs after 1815?

PRACTICE TEST

To help you evaluate your understanding of the lesson, turn to Appendix B and complete the Practice Test for the lesson. The Practice Test contains multiple-choice questions and essay questions, followed by a Feedback Report with correct answers and references.

Lesson 14

Good Feelings and Bad

LESSON ASSIGNMENTS

Review the following assignments in order to schedule your time appropriately. Pay careful attention; the titles and numbers of the textbook chapter, the telecourse guide lesson, and the video program may be different from one another.

Text: Nash et al., *The American People, Volume One: To 1877*, Chapter 9, "Society and Politics in the Early Republic," pp. 289-295 and pp. 309-316 (at "The United States and the Americas").

Video: "Good Feelings and Bad," from the series, *The American Adventure*.

OVERVIEW

The aggressive, expansive, and optimistic feelings of post-war America are traced through foreign affairs, domestic politics, and economic changes. Pensacola, Florida, where Andrew Jackson took possession of the Spanish fort, and Washington, D.C., provide a visual background for this study of the aggressive surge of economic and political policies following the War of 1812. Examined also is the impact the war had on nationalism and sectionalism.

INTRODUCTION

The War of 1812 was over! A great victory had punctuated its end. The exuberance of the youthful republic was dramatically illustrated by an outburst of nationalistic foreign policies. The country was treated with a new respect. Even England preferred compromise to confrontation, which led to a series of negotiated settlements. More dramatically, Spain's declining power was exposed. In a spectacular explosion of energy, Andrew Jackson invaded Spanish Florida in pursuit of Seminole Indians. He captured a few Indians, two gun-running British citizens, and every Spanish fort except St. Augustine.

Although the United States publicly repudiated Jackson's seizure of Florida, Secretary of State John Q. Adams informed the Spanish government it had better control Florida or be prepared to lose it. The result was the Adams-Onís Treaty (Transcontinental Treaty) which gave the United States Florida as well as Spain's claim to Oregon. The United States gave up its claim to Texas and assumed $5 million in American claims against Spain. The United States also issued a ringing declaration in 1823 that the New World was now closed to colonization. Although the United States was not in a position to enforce Monroe's doctrine, no European power was in a position to challenge it for over a quarter of a century.

This nationalism also was evident in domestic politics. The Federalists largely had been discredited because they opposed the war. The Hartford Convention resolutions left then vulnerable to charges of deserting the United States just as victory neared. The Republicans hastened the Federalists' fall by adopting several of their programs. Most noticeably, a Second National Bank was chartered (1815), a protective tariff implemented (1816), and several internal improvement bills were passed (1816-20). By 1820 the Federalist party had all but disappeared, reflecting a short period of political good feelings.

The rapid economic expansion of the period had a greater variety of effects. The availability of new markets for American agricultural and manufactured products stimulated economic activity. After the Tariff of 1816 gave then some protection against British "dumping," American manufacturers prospered. Commercial interests expanded their trade. But the real push was agrarian. The American farmers, North and South, actively acquired more land and aggressively produced more goods. Unfortunately, the financing of these ventures was not always done with care. Many farmers speculated on the assumption that demands for their goods and prices of those goods would escalate higher and higher. They were wrong. European crop productions increased dramatically in 1818-19, and thus demand for American goods declined. As the supply of cotton caught up to the productive capacities of the English and American mills, the price dropped drastically. Then, a change in the policy of the National Bank which required specie payments from state banks started the economy into a sharp, deep deflationary cycle. This decline produced the Panic of 1819. The people caught in the downdraft of debts and foreclosures looked for a scapegoat. The southern and western farmers blamed the eastern bankers, and especially the National Bank. This sectional rift diminished the good feelings of the postwar period.

The rapid expansion of the country after the War of 1812 had another significant result—more states. By 1818, the Union had expanded to twenty-two states. In that year, Missouri sought to become the twenty-third member. It was a pivotal application; it would be the first new area formed from the Louisiana Territory and it straddled the traditional dividing line of slave and free states (i.e., the Ohio River, from the Pennsylvania-Maryland border westward). Missouri wanted to enter as a slave state. A debate raged. Northerners demanded that slavery be stricken from the Missouri Constitution. Southerners reacted with outrage. Eventually, the issue was compromised; the balance between free and slave states was maintained when Missouri was admitted as a slave state and Maine as a free state. In an attempt to avoid future arguments, the Missouri Compromise divided the remaining Louisiana Territory at the 36° 30′ parallel between free and slave territories. But the issue had been raised. Bad feelings emerged. As John Quincy Adams observed, "I take it for granted that the present question is a mere preamble—a title page to a great, tragic volume."

LEARNING OBJECTIVES

Upon completion of the lesson you should develop and be able to demonstrate an understanding of:

1. The significant changes taking place in American commercial, industrial, and agricultural activities.
2. The evidence of a strong nationalistic response to the end of the War of 1812.
3. The evidence of a dangerous sectional trend in economic and social policies in the postwar years.
4. The end of the Federalist-Republican party system.

KEY TERMS

Look for these items as you proceed through the lesson assignments. Be able to define them upon completion of this lesson.

People

John Quincy Adams
Henry Clay
William Crawford
Andrew Jackson

Rufus King
James Madison
James Monroe
Chris Robinson

Places

Appalachian Mountains
Argentina
Chile
Colombia
Derby Wharf, Salem
Florida

Maine
Mexico
Missouri
Pawtucket, Rhode Island
36° 30′
Walthan, Massachusetts

Events and Terms

Boston Associates
cotton gin
corrupt bargain
Embargo Act, 1807
merchant capitalist
Missouri Compromise
Monroe Doctrine

Panic of 1819
Second National Bank of the
United States (BUS)
Second Great Awakening
short staple cotton
Tariff of 1816

Ideas

Old Republicans
protective tariff

universal white male suffrage
Wealth of Nations

TEXT FOCUS POINTS

The following focus points are designed to help you get the most from the text. Review them, then read the assignment. You may want to write notes to reinforce what you have learned.

Text: Nash et al., *The American People*, Chapter 9, pp. 289-295 and 309-316 (at "The United States and the Americas").

1. Why did the United States government not recognize new Latin American republics until 1822?
2. What was the origin of the Monroe Doctrine? What were its tenets?
3. What were the impacts on the Indians of rapid trans-Appalachia immigration of whites? What was the goal of the new Indian policy? Results?
4. What Native American strategies evolved to deal with the rapidly advancing white population in the trans-Appalachian interior?
5. What was the policy of assimilation?
6. How successful was Indian armed resistance? What defeats in the North and South signaled the end of armed resistance?
7. In what ways had the Republicans adopted Federalist (nationalistic) policies following the war?
8. What sectional tensions surfaced in this period?
9. Study the map on page 314. Which states were free and which were slave in 1821? Where was the Louisiana Territory to be divided between free and slave?
10. How were politics changing in the 1820s?
11. How did the election of 1824 help disrupt the Republican party?

VIDEO FOCUS POINTS

The following focus points are designed to help you get the most from the video segment of this lesson. Review them, then watch the video. You may want to write notes to reinforce what you have learned.

Video: "Good Feelings and Bad"

Synopsis: Addresses the exuberant surge of nationalistic foreign policy and economic sectionalism following the war of 1812.

1. Why did Andrew Jackson pursue the Seminole Indians into Florida? What resulted from this attack?
2. What did Professor K. Jack Bauer say that explained the aggressive foreign actions of the United States after the war?
3. What factors were involved in the post-war economic expansion of the country?
4. What was the response of the Bank of the United States (BUS) in 1818 to rapid expansion? What was the result?
5. What did Professor Bauer indicate were the causes of the Panic of 1819? What were its results?

OPTIONAL LEARNING ACTIVITY

Following the War of 1812, the people of the United States experienced a burst of energy and enthusiasm. The results produced tendencies toward both nationalism and sectionalism. In a two-page paper, first describe the incidence of nationalism and sectionalism, and, second, explain how both of these trends could happen simultaneously.

SUGGESTED READINGS

Further readings can be found in the text on pages 316-317.

HISTORICAL PERSPECTIVE

Postwar reactions frequently give impetus to important changes in a country. The War of 1812 was certainly no exception. The pre-war and postwar experiences changed the economic nature of American society, altered the balance of the political parties, intensified nationalistic foreign policies, and gave impetus to sectional differences. Can you compare these results with more recent American postwar periods, such as World War II or Vietnam? Do you find similarities? Differences? How do you explain the significance of the postwar periods?

PRACTICE TEST

To help you evaluate your understanding of the lesson, turn to Appendix B and complete the Practice Test for the lesson. The Practice Test contains multiple-choice questions and essay questions, followed by a Feedback Report with correct answers and references.

Unit Three
Expanding to the Horizons

The United States began with its people on the move, and expansion continued with even greater vigor in the second quarter of the nineteenth century. The country's boundaries and settlements were extended to the Pacific Ocean. Its territories and population doubled. Economically, the country expanded its agricultural wealth and developed new manufacturing and commercial interests. Politically, the republican ideology pushed political participation to all free, white, twenty-one-year-old males, and the new leaders preached the ideals of egalitarianism. The urge to expand the virtues of the country to all its citizens was so great that social ills were attacked with remarkable fervor. Reformers, revivalists, and utopians converged upon the land offering their own brands of redemption. But beneath the hustle and bustle, deep-seated differences threatened the country's survival.

Lesson 15

The Expanding Nation

LESSON ASSIGNMENTS

Review the following assignments in order to schedule your time appropriately. Pay careful attention; the titles and numbers of the textbook chapter, the telecourse guide lesson, and the video program may be different from one another.

Text: Nash, et al., *The American People, Volume One: To 1877,*
Chapter 9, "Society and Politics in the Early Republic," pp. 289-295;
Chapter 10, "Currents of Change in the Northeast and the Old Northwest," pp. 320-357; and
Chapter 12, "Shaping America in the Antebellum Age," pp. 404-405. (read only the paragraphs on Cherokee removal)

Video: "The Expanding Nation,"
from the Series, *The American Adventure.*

OVERVIEW

The expansive forces that were transforming the natural and coastal United States into a regionalized nation stretching to the Mississippi River and beyond are examined. Changes included the rapid growth of industry, commerce, and agriculture in the first half of the nineteenth century. The junction of the Hiawsee and Tennessee Rivers, and Indian Territory In Oklahoma provide scenic background to the bitter story of Indian removal in the face of rapid westward expansion of white people toward the Mississippi River.

INTRODUCTION

Growth and expansion were the prevailing themes during the forty years before the Civil War. The economy was changing and expanding; people were on the move and the population was increasing. The effects of such rapid changes and growth were numerous. Perhaps most noticeable was the development of busy manufacturing/urban centers; the most significant change, the application of machines to labor; and the most tragic consequence, the callous removal of the Indians from their homelands.

The commercial and manufacturing orientation established by the conclusion of the War of 1812 exploded into activity with the advent of peace. Factories with workers on site were becoming the norm. The Lowell girls in the New England textile mills were one form this productive system took. Other industries soon developed and workers crowded into the cities. A whole new culture and way of life emerged.

The diffused population of the United States presented transportation and communication problems. New commercial transportation and communication systems were necessary to distribute factory products. Initially, roads and canals were built. Later, railroads would bind the nation together. The advent of less expensive and more reliable means of moving goods and people expanded the markets for these goods. Western farmers found markets for their products in the northeastern cities. Southern cotton helped fuel New England textile mills. And, of course, the canals and roads were clogged with hopeful settlers looking for land and seeking their fortunes. The seemingly endless lands were filling with remarkable rapidity, and previous ways of life eroded away.

The trans-Appalachian Indian tribes lay in the path of this flood of migrants, so they were removed. Sometimes treaties were negotiated. At other times, wars were fought. In other cases, negotiations failed, courts were ignored, and the Indians were just moved. This drive for land finally forced the Cherokee along a "Trail of Tears." Their land was then available for white settlement.

These changes helped mold America into a country that displayed great diversity and a way of life very different than had been known previously. Regional differences emerged. Each region had connections with the other, but discordant elements also existed. The South wanted eastern markets. They also wanted low tariffs, cheap land, and the protection and expansion of slavery. The West wanted eastern and southern markets and cheap land, but, unlike the South, they wanted protective tariffs and a restraint on the expansion of slavery. The North wanted western and southern goods, but higher land prices, protective tariffs, and restraint on the expansion of slavery.

The changing nation had myriad facades. The old rural values were challenged by new urban realities. The opportunities to apply new technology gradually commercialized the farm and city. Just as significantly, this burst of activity created various needs, attitudes, and environments. This diversity had the potential to shake the nation.

LEARNING OBJECTIVES

Upon completion of this lesson you should develop and be able to demonstrate an understanding of:

1. The trends in American manufacturing and commerce to 1860 and the implications of these changes.
2. The evolving need for the development of national transportation and communication systems.
3. The development of regional identities in the period following the War of 1812.
4. The differences between rural and urban lifestyles in the nineteenth century.
5. The impact of westward migration on the Indians of the Ohio Valley.

KEY TERMS

Look for these items as you proceed through the lesson assignments. Be able to define them upon completion of this lesson.

People

Cherokee Indians	Sequoyah
Creek Indiàns	Shawnee Indians
Francis Cabot Lowell	Smauel Slater
Horace Mann	John Stewart
John Ross	

Continued on next page

Places

Chincinnati, Ohio
Erie Canal
Hiawsee and Tennessee Rivers

Lowell, Massachusetts
Oklahoma

Events and Terms

antebellum
Dartmouth College v. Woodward
Horseshoe Bend
McCormick harvester

Palmer v. Mulligan
Sturges v. Crowinshield
"Trail of Tears"
Worcester v. Georgia

Ideas

accomodation
assimilation
black civil rights

industrialization
middle class
urbanization

TEXT FOCUS POINTS

The following focus points are designed to help you get the most from the text. Review them, then read the assignment. You may want to write notes to reinforce what you have learned.

Text: Nash et al., *The American People*, Chapter 9, pp. 289-295, Chapter 10, pp. 320-357, and Chapter 12, pp. 404-405. (read only the paragraphs on Cherokee removal)

1.   What was the primary objective of federal Indian policy after 1790? How successful was the policy? What impact did this policy have on the Indians? The whites?
2.   What was the Cherokee strategy? What was the final outcome of this strategy? (Read Chapter 12, pp. 404-405.)

3. How did natural and population resources help fuel American economic growth?

4. What role did transportation play in the economic transformation of the United States to 1860?

5. From where did investment capital come?

6. How did the government encourage economic growth?

7. What factors encouraged innovation? What were the reactions to the changes?

8. What role was industrialization playing in this growth? With what environmental consequences?

9. How and why did industrialization affect American life?

10. What was life like in a mill town? What were the roles of women and immigrants in the work force?

11. Compare frontier factories with those in New England. How were they alike and how did they differ?

12. What forces promoted urbanization? What impact did these forces have?

13. What were the class structures and living conditions of the mid-nineteenth century city?

14. What tensions and problems existed in the cities? What role did blacks play in the development of cities?

15. How were rural life and farming changing? What was family life like on the frontier? How did frontier settlement impact the environment?

VIDEO FOCUS POINTS

The following focus points are designed to help you get the most from the video segment of this lesson. Review them, then watch the video. You may want to write notes to reinforce what you have learned.

Video: "The Expanding Nation"

Synopsis: Addresses the changes that came with rapid growth of industry, commerce, and agriculture in the first half of the nineteenth century.

1. How was the country changing during the first half of the nineteenth century?

2. What was life in the Lowell mills like?
3. How was the machine age changing farm life?
4. What main elements of change did Professor Julie Jeffrey point out?
5. Why was it hard to justify removal of the Cherokee? How did it take place?
6. What reasons did Professor R. David Edmunds give for the harsh treatment of the Cherokee and other Indians?

OPTIONAL LEARNING ACTIVITY

In a two-page essay, describe the differences in lifestyle and attitude between rural and urban societies. Identify a particular class level and weave into the narrative how that would affect your perception.

SUGGESTED READINGS

Further readings can be found in the text on pages 357.

HISTORICAL PERSPECTIVE

The consequences of the rapid industrialization and commercialization of the nineteenth century United States had manifold results. Demands for markets and the protection of those markets were made on government. The rise of a large-scale urban working class with little to sell except their labor gave rise to new problems. The urban congestion likewise was new. Even the increasingly commercial attitudes toward farming and making a profit changed that ancient endeavor. How are these changes reflected in the new self-help literature of the period? Is there a relationship between the creation of the ideals of domesticity and the middle class family? How do these new ideals compare to the agrarian ideals of an earlier time? Was the emergence of an industrial-urban society as significant in creating American ideology as our rural past?

PRACTICE TEST

To help you evaluate your understanding of the lesson, turn to Appendix B and complete the Practice Test for the lesson. The Practice Test contains multiple-choice questions and essay questions, followed by a Feedback Report with correct answers and references.

Lesson 16

The South's Slave System

LESSON ASSIGNMENTS

Review the following assignments in order to schedule your time appropriately. Pay careful attention; the titles and numbers of the textbook chapter, the telecourse guide lesson, and the video program may be different from one another.

Text: Nash, et al., *The American People, Volume One: To 1877,* Chapter 11, "Slavery and the Old South," pp. 358-393.

Reader: *Perspectives on America, Volume I,*" Children of Darkness,"by Oates.

Video: "The South's Slave System," from the Series, *The American Adventure.*

OVERVIEW

The ambiance of an antebellum plantation sets the stage for an investigation of slavery as an institution. The different points of view of slave and master are creatively detailed.

INTRODUCTION

Slavery was a labor and social system, demanding its own political arrangements. Never has an institutional pattern been so pervasive, insidious, and dangerous to the American people and society. It evolved as a means of creating a laboring class which allowed whites to compete for wealth and freedom.

The legal foundations of the South's slave system were the slave codes. These bodies of regulations clearly established white superiority before the law. The codes gave slaveowners nearly absolute control of their laborers' activities and made

---

all black slaves subservient to all white people. But slavery's primary purpose was to create an efficient labor system. The slaves had to establish whatever cultural, social, and intellectual order they could from within the system.

Slave owning was not universal in the South. More than seventy-five percent of the white families owned no slaves. The vast majority of slaveholders held but a few slaves, seventy percent holding ten or less. However, the very large planters that used the labor of hundreds of slaves had vast economic, social, and political influence. Yet, the non-slaveholders believed in the plantation ideal and dreamed of becoming one of the great landowners.

The physical brutality of the system generally was not random or purposeless. The events that most frequently involved brutality were slave insurrections or fear of them, the capture of runaways, punishment of crimes, and slave trading. Elements of physical brutality were the natural accompaniment of all of these situations. Sadistic and cruel owners sometimes abused slaves for little or no reason, but such owners were not common and generally were ostracized by the other planters.

Slave work varied widely. The most common responsibilities centered on production and field work. These field hands were at the bottom of the plantation hierarchy. Skills such as blacksmithing, tool repair, coachman, and animal care were much more highly prized. At the top of the slave hierarchy were the household slaves. These individuals walked the difficult path between running the master's house, maintaining their family, and ordering other slaves. They were frequently the most trusted while, at the same time, most aware of the whites' affairs. No matter what position the slaves held, if they did not perform as expected, they would be punished as severely as the owner deemed necessary.

Even with all the restrictions and inhibiting factors, a true black culture emerged. Religion was one major element of the inner life of slavery. The formal worship sanctioned by the master frequently was barely tolerated by the slaves. Their own church meetings were more poignant and sufficing emotional appeals for deliverance from the fear and dread of their everyday life. They released pent-up energy by singing and dancing. The words of the spiritual music had hidden meanings, and thus, acted as coded and subversive communications. Similarly, the slaves used folktales and stories to bolster their self-image and to transfer their hostility. The family provided another source of support that helped the slaves endure. They established and maintained these ties as best they could. These cultural developments helped them fight against their bondage in every way they could without suffering additional punishment.

The slave system influenced the white community in numerous ways. It gave them a narrow vision of work and society. The kindest of husbands and fathers could be brutal when dealing with the slave workers. Such absolute control bred a dictatorial spirit and a militant combativeness. A deep racial antipathy was a natural outgrowth of the South's plantation system. The legacy of those attitudes remained virulent for many decades after slavery's end.

Slavery lingered in the South, locking the section into an economic and intellectual web. The more old-fashioned and outdated the institution became, the more tightly it was held onto. The critical difference between the South and the other sections of the country was, at root, the difference between the demands of a slave society versus those of a competitive capitalist society.

LEARNING OBJECTIVES

Upon completion of the lesson you should develop and be able to demonstrate an understanding of:

1. The rapid expansion of the cotton crop and its implications for slavery.
2. The multifaceted relationships of masters and slaves.
3. The cultural patterns of blacks in slavery including religion, storytelling, and family life.
4. The ways blacks resisted slavery.
5. The status and roles of free blacks.

KEY TERMS

Look for these items as you proceed through the lesson assignments. Be able to define them upon completion of this lesson.

People

Adele Petigree Allston.
Robert F. W. Allston
J. D. B. DeBow

Frederick Douglass
Nat Turner

Continued on next page

Place

cotton belt

Events and Terms

antebellum   free blacks
Brer Fox   overseer
Brer Rabbit   poor whites
Brer Wolf   slave trade
DeBow's Review   yeoman farmer
folktales

Idea

subversive literature

TEXT FOCUS POINTS

The following focus points are designed to help you get the most from the text. Review them, then read the assignment. You may want to write notes to reinforce what you have learned.

Text: Nash et al., *The American People,* Chapter 11, pp. 358-393.

1. How was the South able to be composed of diverse interests and areas and yet retain a sectional unity?
2. How had cotton come to dominate southern agriculture? What effect did it have on migration of whites and blacks?
3. What does the map on page 365 show about the economic development of the South to 1860? What was the role of cotton? The role of agriculture in general?
4. How were slaves used in southern production?
5. According to the map on page 366, where were the greatest concentrations of slaves in the antebellum South? Where were the lowest concentrations?

6. What was the overall social structure of the South? What were the various classes' attitudes toward slavery and blacks?
7. How did owning slaves affect whites' work, responsibilities, and ideas?
8. What was the labor of slaves like? How did it affect their health?
9. What was the position of the blacks and their families before the law?
10. What were the characteristics of the slaves' religion? Spirituals? Family?
11. How did blacks resist slavery?
12. What were the lives of free blacks like?

READER FOCUS POINTS

Reader: *Perspectives on America, Volume I* "Children of Darkness," by Oates.

1. By southern, white standards, why were Southampton County, Virginia slave holders enlightened?
2. What influences did Nat Turner's parents have on him? What confused Nat Turner as he came of age?
3. How did religion and the obvious inconsistencies between Christianity and slavery affect Turner?
4. What prompted Nat Turner to strike out against slavery? How did his rebellion work out? What resulted?
5. What resulted from Gray's interview with Nat Turner? What were the consequences of Turner's Rebellion?

VIDEO FOCUS POINTS

The following focus points are designed to help you get the most from the video segment of this lesson. Review them, then watch the video. You may want to write notes to reinforce what you have learned.

Video: "The South's Slave System"

Synopsis: Addresses the lives of slaves and the social/economic relationships established in the antebellum South.

1. What was the purpose of the slave codes?
2. What were fears, hopes, experiences, and perceptions of Hector's father, Munsey, Hector, Virgie, Munsey's mother, and Hector's mother?
3. How did Professor Alphine Jefferson explain the harshness and inflexibility of the slave system?
4. How did Professor Jefferson interpret black spirituals and folktales?

OPTIONAL LEARNING ACTIVITY

The differences in perceptions of events and ideas between slave and master is startling. Write a two- to three-page imaginative essay comparing and contrasting a slave's and master's understanding of the same event, such as marriage, the death of a master or a slave sale. Why are their views different? Who has the clearer perception?

SUGGESTED READINGS

Further readings can be found in the text on pages 392-393.

HISTORICAL PERSPECTIVE

Slavery was the root of the South's sectionalism. It promoted greater and greater concentrations of wealth while at the same time it curtailed economic diversification. Could the South have voluntarily ended slavery and established some form of tenant farming and industrialization? Such a change would have required incredible insight and planning. Had the southern states followed such a path, do you believe race relations and changes in the social and economic status of blacks would have been retarded more than they were? Had the United States followed such a course, possibly the Union of South Africa and the U.S. might be simultaneously facing massive racial unrest in the last decades of the twentieth century!

PRACTICE TEST

To help you evaluate your understanding of the lesson, turn to Appendix B and complete the Practice Test for the lesson. The Practice Test contains multiple-choice questions and essay questions, followed by a Feedback Report with correct answers and references.

Lesson 17

The Jacksonian Persuasion

LESSON ASSIGNMENTS

Review the following assignments in order to schedule your time appropriately. Pay careful attention; the titles and numbers of the textbook chapter, the telecourse guide lesson, and the video program may be different from one another.

Text: Nash, et al., *The American People, Volume One: To 1877*,
          Chapter 12, "Shaping America in the Antebellum Age," pp. 398-409.

Reader: *Perspectives on America, Volume I*, "The Debts We Never Paid," by
          Wernick.

Video: "The Jacksonian Persuasion,"
          from the Series, *The American Adventure*.

OVERVIEW

A country store in the West and picturesque Charleston, South Carolina provide settings for Jacksonian politics. The political ingredients of the new politics and the crisis over nullification give insights into Jacksonian America. Special focus is on Andrew Jackson and the implications and results of the growing democratization of American politics in the second quarter of the nineteenth century.

INTRODUCTION

The social and economic pressures that were changing America also had a powerful impact on politics, religion, and reform. The political scene would never be the same. The increasing number of eligible voters, and a greater awareness and

---

interest in politics, combined to give the average man a larger role in governing. The central figure and symbol of the new politics was Andrew Jackson. His military victories over the Indians and British made him well-known and popular. That such qualities could be used for political gain, despite a poor education and little previous political experience, was indeed new.

Jackson re-entered politics following his victories at New Orleans and Pensacola. He was chosen Senator from Tennessee and then had his name placed on many ballots for president in 1824. His defeat in the split vote of that election convinced him of a need for a people's president and a reorganization of the political system. Substantial support gathered around him. In 1828 the electoral results were reversed from 1824, and he ascended to the presidency.

Jackson believed the president, more than any other official, represented all the people. He left an indelible imprint of his personality and attitudes on the United States government. From the moment of his inauguration when the "common" people celebrated wildly, to his personal attack on the "monster bank," he acted in a direct and decisive way.

Jackson confronted the established bureaucracy by removing opposing party appointees and replacing them with loyal Democrats. He faced the challenge of nullification with directness and boldness. The hostility of supporters of the Bank of the United States inspired him to a frenzy of activity resulting in the destruction of the Bank. He may not always have realized the results of his actions, but he always acted with purpose. He left office loved by the common people, and he left the nation a new model of presidential politics.

The floodtide of Jacksonian politics changed the party system. The powerful, new Democratic party with its clever organization and campaign techniques forced the opposition to create a similar organization. By 1836 the Whig party was structured, and the new competitive system was complete. The competitive, rapidly changing society had spawned a political system with the same characteristics. Now, any American could run for political office; no longer did just the elite stand for election.

LEARNING OBJECTIVES

Upon completion of the lesson you should develop and be able to demonstrate an understanding of:

1. The changes in American political procedures and behavior during the "Jacksonian Period."
2. The nullification concept and controversy and its implications for the United States.
3. The controversy between Andrew Jackson and the supporters of the Bank of the United States.
4. The new party system that had evolved by 1836.
5. Martin Van Buren's presidency.

KEY TERMS

Look for these items as you proceed through the lesson assignments. Be able to define them upon completion of this lesson.

People

John Q. Adams	Andrew Jackson
Francis Blair	Amos Kendall
Nicholas Biddle	Roger Taney
John C. Calhoun	John Tyler
Henry Clay	Martin Van Buren
William Henry Harrison	Daniel Webster

Places

Cumberland Gap	Wilderness Road

Events and Terms

American System	National Republican party

Continued on next page

Anti-Masonic party	Nullification Crisis
Democratic party	"Old Hickory"
Exposition and Protest	Specie Circular
"King mob"	Tariff of Abomination
kitchen cabinet	Whig party

Ideas

nullification   Jacksonian Democracy

TEXT FOCUS POINTS

The following focus points are designed to help you get the most from the text. Review them, then read the assignment. You may want to write notes to reinforce what you have learned.

Text: Nash et al., *The American People,* Chapter 12, pp. 398-409.

1. What changes were affecting American political culture in the 1820s and 1830s?
2. What was Andrew Jackson's personal and political background? How did his candidacy for president reflect a change in the political system? How were the changes reflected in the 1828 election?
3. What were Jackson's views of the presidency? How did he use its powers in regard to appointments and Indians?
4. What positions were crystallizing regarding tariffs? How was nullification related to this question? What resulted when South Carolina "nullified" the tariff?
5. Why did Jackson attack the Bank of the United States? What happened when he did? What was the impact on Martin Van Buren's presidency?
6. What reorganization took place in the "party" system during Jackson's presidency? What was the result?
7. What did the election of 1840 reveal about the new political campaigns?

READER FOCUS POINTS

Reader: *Perspectives on America, Volume I*, "The Debts We Never Paid," by Wernick.

1. Why had American states borrowed heavily in the 1820s and 1830s? Why did these practices lead to trouble in the 1840s?
2. How did the states react to these debts, especially the eight defaulting states?

VIDEO FOCUS POINTS

The following focus points are designed to help you get the most from the video segment of this lesson. Review them, then watch the video. You may want to write notes to reinforce what you have learned.

Video: "The Jacksonian Persuasion"

Synopsis: Discusses Andrew Jackson and the democratization of American politics.

1. What qualities of the West did Andrew Jackson exemplify?
2. What factors did Professor Edward Pessen identify as critical to the rise of Jacksonianism? Were they really democratic?
3. What were the characteristics of the election of 1828? Why did Jackson win?
4. How did the politics surrounding the central government change due to the election of Jackson, according to Professor Pessen?
5. What was nullification? What crisis was precipitated by its attempted implementation?
6. In his analysis, what did Professor Pessen say about the quick solution to the nullification crisis?

OPTIONAL LEARNING ACTIVITY

If you were running for office in rural Tennessee in the 1830s, what would be most appealing about you to the electorate? Write a two-page campaign plan. Describe how you would "sell" yourself to the voters. What would be your stand on banking, the tariff, and land sales?

SUGGESTED READINGS

Further readings can be found in the text on pages 430-431. Of special interest is *Jacksonian America: Society, Personalty and Politics* by Edward Pessen.

HISTORICAL PERSPECTIVE

During the Jacksonian Period, American politics were altered. What were the most significant changes from previous policies? What were the long-term implications of the new political methodology? Were the long-term results beneficial or detrimental to the quality of government? Why? What was the role of Andrew Jackson in this process? As a milestone in the continuing democratization of the political process, how significant was this period?

PRACTICE TEST

To help you evaluate your understanding of the lesson, turn to Appendix B and complete the Practice Test for the lesson. The Practice Test contains multiple-choice questions and essay questions, followed by a Feedback Report with correct answers and references.

Lesson 18

Reforming the Republic

LESSON ASSIGNMENTS

Review the following assignments in order to schedule your time appropriately. Pay careful attention; the titles and numbers of the textbook chapter, the telecourse guide lesson, and the video program may be different from one another.

Text: Nash et al., *The American People, Volume One: To 1877,*
           Chapter 12, "Shaping America in the Antebellum Age," pp. 394-398 and
           pp. 410-431.

Reader: *Perspectives on America, Volume I*, "Pentecosts in the Backwoods," by
          Weisberger.

Video: "Reforming the Republic,"
           from the series, *The American Adventure*.

OVERVIEW

The weaving together of urges for revivalism and reform is the focus of the program. The locations include a revival camp meeting site, a Massachusetts commune, a Boston abolitionist's church, and Elizabeth Cady Stanton's home. The dynamic changes taking place in the religious, philosophic, and reform activities of Jacksonian America are studied.

INTRODUCTION

The dynamics of Jacksonian America left a tremendous impression on the social and religious texture of the United States. The dogmatic Calvinism of the colonial Puritans and Edwardian Awakening gave way to the more optimistic and activist

---

Second Great Awakening of the nineteenth century. Revivalists, whether in rural camp meetings or urban tents, promoted a religious perspective that called on the masses to actively pursue their own salvation and carry on the Christian work. It was a hopeful plea based on the assumption that people could effect their own destiny. It was a demanding plea in that it required a commitment to work. The denominations proliferated, and the messages varied, but the direction was always the same— "people save yourselves and remold American society into a heaven on earth."

Of all the new movements, none was more militant or dynamic than the Mormons'. The Mormon movement created a community of believers who followed their leaders to the Great Salt Flats. Their appeal was for individuals willing to commit to the rigorous demands of a community life dominated by religion.

Just as the religious responses to Jacksonian egalitarian theory varied, so did the social responses. The reformers perceived a society that fell well short of its lofty ideals, a society that was all movement and change. Their concerns included education, abolition, women's rights, temperance, prisons, and asylums. Publications, agitation, and confrontation were common means used by the reformers to try to win their way. A few tried to accomplish a purer society by forming their own special communities of like-thinking people. These utopian communitarians began with lofty goals and principles, but inevitably broke up on the rocks of individualism and dissension. Rarely has the United States experienced such an intense period of reform activity. Although few of the goals were fully realized, the Jacksonian reformers set a substantial agenda for later generations.

The philosophic response to the dynamics of the period was exemplified by Ralph Waldo Emerson and the transcendentalists. Beginning with the "romantic" assumptions of humanity's innate goodness and the higher value of intuition and emotion for discovering truth, these writers, thinkers, and teachers started new and lasting intellectual trends. Henry David Thoreau made an emotional and intuitive appeal for a return to nature, and even stood up against the war-making power of the federal government.

The elements of a diverse, fragmented, multifaceted America had emerged. The homogeneous, agrarian America of the past was irretrievably gone, and, for better or worse, the new America was at hand.

LEARNING OBJECTIVES

Objectives—Upon completion of the lesson you should develop and be able to demonstrate an understanding of:

1. The changes in American religious life during the Jacksonian Period.
2. The influence and significance of the transcendentalist.
3. The nature and significance of the Utopian movements.
4. The major reforms, leaders, and movements of the period.

KEY TERMS

Look for these items as you proceed through the lesson assignments. Be able to define them upon completion of this lesson.

People

Adin Ballou	Lucretia Mott
Martin Delany	John Humphrey Noyes
Dorothea Dix	Emily Robinson
Frederick Douglass	Marius Robinson
Ralph Waldo Emerson	Joseph Smith
Charles G. Finney	Elizabeth Cady Stanton
William Lloyd Garrison	Henry David Thoreau
Angelina Grimké	Sojourner Truth
Sarah Grimké	Theodore Dwight Weld
Abby Kelley	Brigham Young
Mother Ann Lee	

Places

Brook Farm	New Harmony
camp meeting	Oneida
Hopedale	Rochester

Continued on next page

Events and Terms

abolition	Mormons
American Anti-Slavery Society	Phalanx
asylum reform	revivals
Shakers	health manuals
gag rule	Temperance
The Liberator	Transcendentalism (ists)
Millerites	

Ideas

Calivinistic tenets	intuition
communalism	moral free agents

TEXT FOCUS POINTS

The following focus points are designed to help you get the most from the text. Review them, then read the assignment. You may want to write notes to reinforce what you have learned.

Text: Nash et al., *The American People,* Chapter 12, pp. 394-398 and pp. 410-431.

1. What role did Charles Finney play in the Second Great Awakening?
2. How had the location of intense revivalism shifted from the early 1800s to the 1830s? What were the theological emphases of the preachers?
3. What were the major impulses that promoted reformist activism? (Note the table on p. 412.)
4. What were the dilemmas of reformers?
5. What was Ralph Waldo Emerson's role in intellectualizing the need for reform? How did Hawthorne and Melville reflect similar attitudes? What was Henry David Thoreau's role?
6. What were the goals, leaders, and experiences of the various utopian communities?

---

7. Who were the Millerites and the Mormons?
8. Using the map on page 417, where were the Mormon settlements? Where were Brook Farm, Oneida, New Harmony, and Seneca Falls?
9. Why was temperance such a critical issue? What were the goals of the movement?
10. What problems of health and sexuality were addressed? What impact did these changes have on daily living?
11. Who worked tirelessly for asylum reform? For education reform?
12. What goals did the working class move toward?
13. Who were the leading abolitionists? What were their goals, methods, and influence? How did the anti-abolitionists counterattack?
14. Who were the leaders of the women's rights movement? What did they advocate? With what results?

READER FOCUS POINTS

Reader: *Perspectives on America, Volume I,* "Pentecosts in the Backwoods," by Weisberger.

1. What role did religion play to the early nineteenth century westerner?
2. What role did James McGready play in creating a religion for the West? What others followed him with what results?
3. How did the camp meeting revivals get started? What happened at Cane Ridge? With what results?
4. What was the "third act" in the development of the revivals?
5. How did the eastern churches eventually react to the new revivalism?

VIDEO FOCUS POINTS

The following focus points are designed to help you get the most from the video segment of this lesson. Review them, then watch the video. You may want to write notes to reinforce what you have learned.

Video: "Reforming the Republic"

Synopsis: Addresses the impact of revivalism, abolition, and women's rights in nineteenth century America.

1. What were the messages of the revivalists?
2. How did Professor Harvey Graff interrelate the three elements of economic, political, and social change of the Jacksonian Period?
3. What were the Utopians' intentions? What were the results of their efforts?
4. What were the goals of the abolitionists? How did the public react to these people and their messages?
5. What were the goals and concerns of the women's rights leaders? How were they received?
6. What similarities and differences did Professor Graff describe between the women's rights and abolitionist movements?

OPTIONAL LEARNING ACTIVITIES

1. Choose a reform movement other than abolition or women's rights and write a two page paper describing its central concerns and important leaders. What successes did the advocates have? What problems and opposition did they encounter?
2. The use of travel journals as a source of information about American society is explored in the text article on pages 402-03. Carefully read and evaluate the three separate entries in a two-page essay. What differences in perception did you note? Which seemed most favorable toward the American society? Which was most critical? Do their observations seem to have any relevance to contemporary American society? Why or why not?

SUGGESTED READINGS

Further readings can be found in the text on pages 430-431.

HISTORICAL PERSPECTIVE

Jacksonian Democrats were not very interested in reform. Yet, the same egalitarian and ideological forces which enlarged the electorate and elected Democrats also provided the impetus for social changes. How can these divergences be explained? Why do responses to social changes vary by class, region, and personality? Do you believe the reformers really wanted equality for others? Why or why not?

PRACTICE TEST

To help you evaluate your understanding of the lesson, turn to Appendix B and complete the Practice Test for the lesson. The Practice Test contains multiple-choice questions and essay questions, followed by a Feedback Report with correct answers and references.

Lesson 19

Manifest Destiny

LESSON ASSIGNMENTS

Review the following assignments in order to schedule your time appropriately. Pay careful attention; the titles and numbers of the textbook chapter, the telecourse guide lesson, and the video program may be different from one another.

Text: Nash, et al., *The American People, Volume One: To 1877*, Chapter 13, "Moving West," pp. 432-469.

Reader: *Perspectives on America, Volume I*, "The Thankless Task of Nicholas Trist," by Ketchum.

Video: "Manifest Destiny," from the Series, *The American Adventure*.

OVERVIEW

The concept of Manifest Destiny is described and its implications for war and diplomacy are examined. Barren deserts, pine woods, sea coasts, and prairies combined to form the lands the United States coveted.

INTRODUCTION

As the United States entered the fourth and fifth decades of the nineteenth century, its people continued to move west into new territory. The limits of settlements were pushed from the Appalachians to the Mississippi, and then across the Great River all the way to the Pacific Ocean. This prodigious onslaught of humanity accepted no limitations and no barriers to their expansion goals. Soon the whole country seemed to be caught up in a frenzy of growth. Americans believed it was a "Manifest

Destiny" of the Almighty that America overspread the continent. Unfortunately for peace and harmony, the lands the Americans wanted were already occupied. The Mexican Republic claimed the lands from Texas to the Pacific; England had a strong hold on the Oregon Territory to Alaska; and Native Americans were spread throughout the West.

The active acquisition of the lands coveted by the United States was precipitated by the election of 1844. The Whigs chose aging Henry Clay who lukewarmly espoused expansionism. The Democrats forsook their better known hopefuls to nominate James Knox Polk of Tennessee. Polk was an avowed expansionist. The Democratic party platform called for the acquisition of all the Oregon Territory to Alaska, all of California, and the annexation of Texas. When Polk won, he seemed to have a mandate to fulfill Manifest Destiny. Although he almost blundered out of an agreement with Great Britain, Polk did send to the Senate a compromise giving the United States all of continental Oregon south of the forty-ninth parallel. In dealing with a powerful England, Polk was prepared to compromise.

Unfortunately for Mexico, Polk was much more aggressive in dealing with a weaker country. The annexation of Texas was begun by President Tyler as he left office, but was completed after Polk took office in 1845. He tried to buy the territory west from Texas to the Pacific, but his offer was rejected. Negotiations failing, he had General Zachary Taylor march his troops into disputed territory on the north side of the Rio Grande River. The Mexican Army reacted, and on April 24, 1846, advanced across the river. The next day blood was spilled. Polk then appealed to the Congress for war; it was declared.

The Mexican-American War was relatively short. The United States acquitted itself well militarily. Taylor moved from the Rio Grande south. Later, Winfield Scott led a remarkable amphibious landing followed by an unprecedented advance to the Mexican capital. The war was ended by the Treaty of Guadalupe Hidalgo which achieved all of Polk's pre-war aims.

These lands provided a bonanza for would-be settlers. The movement west had accelerated after independence, increased more after the War of 1812, and now in the 1830s and 1840s, reached tremendous proportions. The goal of settlement was still the same: to improve one's position in life. The places and means varied. The settlers frequently moved much greater distances than were normal in the settling of the Ohio River Valley. The discovery of gold in California and subsequently in other western areas stimulated a very different kind of settlement experience. Americans were on the move.

Because much of the land out West was already occupied, conflict and bloodshed were unavoidable. The Indian and Mexican settlers were rudely displaced. The Indians were pushed and moved into smaller and smaller portions of their domains. The Mexicans were discriminated against and afforded second-class citizenship. For these peoples, the American drive west was a disaster.

"Purposeful Polk" had achieved in four years, the one term he had planned, most of the territorial ambitions of the Democratic platform. The powerful, young Republic had seized a third of its weaker neighbor's land. Would the colonial success be the beginning of peace and prosperity? Or, would rancor and controversy over the prizes destroy the country from within?

LEARNING OBJECTIVES

Upon completion of the lesson you should develop and be able to demonstrate an understanding of:

1. The lands the United States sought to acquire to fulfill its "Manifest Destiny."
2. How the United States acquired Oregon, Texas, California, and the Mexican Cession lands.
3. The nature of the Mexican-American War and its outcome.
4. The nature and the impact of antebellum settlement to the Pacific Ocean.

KEY TERMS

Look for these items as you proceed through the lesson assignments. Be able to define them upon completion of this lesson.

People

Stephen Austin

Henry Clay

Antonio Lopez de Santa Anna

General Winfield Scott

Continued on next page

Creek Indians
Sam Houston
Colonel Stephen W. Kearney
John L. O'Sullivan
Plains Indians
James Knox Polk

Sioux Indians
John L. Slidell
Joseph Smith
General Zachary Taylor
John Tyler
Brigham Young

Places

California
California Trail
New Mexico Territory
Nueces River
Oregon Territory
Oregon Trail

Rio Grande River
Salt Lake City
San Francisco
Santa Fe Trail
Texas
Utah Territory

Events and Terms

The Alamo
Battle of San Jacinto
54° 40′
Fort Laramie Council
ghost town
gold rush
Treaty of Guadalupe Hidalgo

Gwinn Land Law
Homestead Act
Lone Star Republic
mining frontier
Mormon
polygamy
urban frontier

Ideas

geographic mobility

Manifest Destiny

TEXT FOCUS POINTS

The following focus points are designed to help you get the most from the text. Review them, then read the assignment. You may want to write notes to reinforce what you have learned.

Text: Nash et al., *The American People,* Chapter 13, pp. 432-469.

1. What kinds of American settlers were already in the trans-Mississippi lands by 1830?
2. Who owned the vast trans-Mississippi lands coveted by the Americans in the 1830s and 1840s?
3. The map on page 438 shows the United States and its territory in 1860. Which acquisitions included Utah, New Mexico, Oregon, Washington, and Minnesota Territories?
4. What is Manifest Destiny?
5. How and why had Texas become an independent republic by 1836?
6. What were the three boundaries of Texas outlined on the map on page 439?
7. How did the Texas question explode during the 1844 election? How did it merge with the issue of Manifest Destiny?
8. How and why did war break out with Mexico? What were the major military events of the war? What were the results of the war?
9. Using the map on page 443, locate the American victories at Matamoros, Monterrey, Buena Vista, Vera Cruz, and Mexico City. Where is Corpus Christi (the site of the Nueces River)?
10. How did Polk solve the Oregon question?
11. How and why did people move to the Far West in the 1830s, 1840s, and 1850s?
12. What trails did the settlers follow?
13. Using the maps on pages 444 and 451, where was the boundary of the Oregon Territory established in 1846? Where were the Santa Fe, Oregon, and California Trails, and the Mormon Trek?
14. What do the maps on page 448 show about the advancing population of the United States?
15. What was life like on the western agricultural, mining, and Mormon frontiers?

16. What were the characteristics of the western urban areas?
17. What impact did the westward movement have on the Indians? What was the Fort Laramie council?
18. What happened to the Mexicans in the western lands?

READER FOCUS POINTS

Reader: *Perspectives on America, Volume I*, "The Thankless Task of Nicholas Trist," by Ketchum.

1. Why did Polk select Nicholas Trist for the tricky and politically explosive role of peace negotiator to end the Mexican-American War? What was he suppose to do?
2. How did Trist and General Scott initially get along? How were their differences overcome?
3. Why was Trist to come home in the fall of 1847? Why did Trist decide to ignore his recall and write a treaty with Mexico?
4. What did President Polk do with the treaty negotiated by Trist? What did he do to Trist?

VIDEO FOCUS POINTS

The following focus points are designed to help you get the most from the video segment of this lesson. Review them, then watch the video. You may want to write notes to reinforce what you have learned.

Video: "Manifest Destiny"

Synopsis: Addresses the impact of mid-nineteenth century westward movement on American-Mexican relations.

1. What were the characteristics of the new settlers moving West in the mid-nineteenth century?

2. How and why did war erupt between Mexico and the American settlers in Texas?
3. How did Professor K. Jack Bauer explain the Americans' attitudes toward expansion?
4. How was the Oregon question settled?
5. Why did war break out between the United States and Mexico? What was the most spectacular campaign?
6. According to Professor Bauer, what was significant about the Mexican-American War?

OPTIONAL LEARNING ACTIVITY

In a two-page paper analyze the use of private historical sources as outlined on pages 446-447 in the text. What are the major strengths and weaknesses of such sources? What do the two excerpts reveal about traveling west in the mid-nineteenth century? What information can be learned about sex roles from each? How are the two accounts similar? How are the two different?

SUGGESTED READINGS

Further readings can be found in the text on page 468-469.

HISTORICAL PERSPECTIVE

The conquest of the American West is generally portrayed as the gallant movement of sturdy settlers into virtually unoccupied territory. Yet, the acquisition and settlement of the Mid and Far West was especially costly. It cost the Native Americans much of their ancestral lands, and thousands their lives. The Mexican settlers lost their national identity, culture and, frequently, their lands and citizenship. Perhaps the highest price was paid by the struggling Mexican nation. The war with the United States cost it one-third of its territory, much national respect, and many thousands of lives. In comparison, the British merely lost control of a territory for which they had little use, but secured their claim to land of continuing value for their citizens. And the United States, although losing several thousand troops and tens of millions of dollars, acquired control of one-third of the continental United States. It seemed a great victory for the Americans, but the two decades following 1849 revealed that the prize came at a very great price.

PRACTICE TEST

To help you evaluate your understanding of the lesson, turn to Appendix B and complete the Practice Test for the lesson. The Practice Test contains multiple-choice questions and essay questions, followed by a Feedback Report with correct answers and references.

Unit Four
If This Union . . . Endure

The fires of sectional controversy erupted once again in the late 1840s and continued throughout the 1850s. The disputes over slavery and slavery's expansion finally led to civil war. This enormous struggle consumed the nation's energy and resources for four difficult and bloody years. In its aftermath were conflicts over political reabsorption of the Confederate states, and the economic and social make up of the postwar South. The nation did indeed endure, but was left with legacies of racial and sectional hatreds that continued into its second century.

Lesson 20

Agitation and Compromise

LESSON ASSIGNMENTS

Review the following assignments in order to schedule your time appropriately. Pay careful attention; the titles and numbers of the textbook chapter, the telecourse guide lesson, and the video program may be different from one another.

Text: Nash, et al., *The American People, Volume One: To 1877*, Chapter 14, "The Union in Peril," pp. 470-481.

Video: "Agitation and Compromise," from the Series, *The American Adventure*.

OVERVIEW

The Mexican Cession lands and the Old Senate Chamber reflect the contrast of the debates and the debated. The problems caused by the expansion of slavery into new territories brought the Union perilously close to conflict in 1850.

INTRODUCTION

The Mexican War was over. Still to be solved, however, were critical problems surrounding the absorption of what was won. Public opinion had been divided over the war, and those divisions became more pronounced as the issues of territorial status and statehood came before the Congress. As early as 1846, Pennsylvania Congressman David Wilmot proposed the prohibition of slavery in all lands west of Texas. The South protested vigorously. In the ensuing four years fraught with agitation, a compromise was at last achieved. For the last time, the United States would find an accommodation between slave and anti-slave advocates.

Certainly compromise was not automatic during these hectic times. Southern radicals were demanding federal protection of slavery in all territories as a property right. Moderates on both sides sifted through proposals advocating popular sovereignty, extending the Missouri Compromise line, or referring the question to the Supreme Court. No one position commanded a majority. But until settlement and statehood were at stake, no solution was necessary. The application of California for statehood in 1848 forced the whole issue into the public arena.

California's need for statehood was undeniable. The influx of gold crazed Americans, the instability of post war rule, and the rapidly increasing population were reasons enough. But, with few slaves and no strong pro slave sentiment, California proposed to enter as a free state. The balance between free and slave states was clearly in jeopardy. Few territories suitable for slave habitation remained, unless the Mexican Cession lands were opened to slavery or Texas divided into several states. Southern leaders perceived the issue as critical to their continued participation in the Union.

Over this issue, the old triumvirate of Clay, Webster, and Calhoun met their last great public challenge. Clay again sought accommodation by offering something for everyone. Eventually five elements of Clay's proposal were pushed through Congress by Stephen Douglas, and a compromise was secured. But the political bonds were so weakened that the next assault risked the unity of the nation. Uncertainty over the future of the Union escalated and fear for its continuation was great.

LEARNING OBJECTIVES

Upon completion of the lesson you should develop and be able to demonstrate an understanding of:

1. The relationship between the territories acquired from Mexico and the question of slavery expansion into those lands.
2. The various proposals for dealing with the question of slavery expansion and how they affected the 1848 election.
3. The terms of the Compromise of 1850, the means by which it was passed, and its effects.

KEY TERMS

Look for these items as you proceed through the lesson assignments. Be able to define them upon completion of this lesson.

People

John C. Calhoun

Lewis Cass

Henry Clay

Stephen Douglas

Frederick Douglass

Millard Fillmore

Free Soil party

Harriet Beecher Stowe

General Zachary Taylor

Sojourner Truth

Daniel Webster

David Wilmot

Places

New Mexico Territory

Utah Territory

Events and Terms

Fugitive Slave Act, 1850

popular sovereignty

36° 30´

Uncle Tom's Cabin

Wilmot Proviso

Idea

secession

TEXT FOCUS POINTS

The following focus points are designed to help you get the most from the text. Review them, then read the assignment. You may want to write notes to reinforce what you have learned.

Text: Nash et al., *The American People*, Chapter 14, pp. 470-481.

1. What was the Wilmot Proviso? What other positions were taken on the issue of slavery in the territories?
2. What significant changes resulted from the election of 1848?
3. What brought the issue of territorial slavery directly before Congress? Explain.
4. What were Clay's proposals for solving the major issues? What happened to his proposals?
5. What areas that Texas claimed were made part of Utah and New Mexico Territories (map, page 478)? Where was the slave trade prohibited by the Compromise of 1850?
6. Who led the passage of the Compromise provisions through Congress? What were the final elements of compromise? What were the consequences of passage?
7. What was the significance of *Uncle Tom's Cabin?*

VIDEO FOCUS POINTS

The following focus points are designed to help you get the most from the video segment of this lesson. Review them, then watch the video. You may want to write notes to reinforce what you have learned.

Video: "Agitation and Compromise"

Synopsis: Addresses the sectional divisions arising over the issue of extending slavery and the passage of the Compromise of 1850.

1. Why were American legislators agitated when Congress convened in 1849?

---

2. Why did the argument over expanding slavery into the western territories seem so foolish?
3. What reasons did Professor Eric Foner give for the heated debate over slavery extension?
4. What were the positions of Clay, Webster, and Calhoun on compromise?
5. According to Professor Foner, why did the compromise finally pass?

OPTIONAL ACTIVITY

Read carefully the excerpts from Clay, Calhoun, and Webster on pages 476-477 in the textbook. Also listen carefully to the speeches in the dramatic illustrated piece in Program 20. In a two page paper answer the following: On what grounds did Clay and Webster defend the Union? Why did Calhoun reject compromise? What do their speeches reveal about their political motivations? Which speech had the greatest impact upon you? Why?

SUGGESTED READINGS

Further readings can be found in the text on pages 502-503. Of special interest is *Free Soil, Free Labor, Free Men* by Eric Foner.

HISTORICAL PERSPECTIVE

The United States confronted an explosive issue in 1850. If not for the unexpected demise of President Taylor, no compromise was likely to have passed in 1850. Could the issues have brought the country to secession and possible Civil War then? Of course that is impossible to know, but certainly the leading characters and the issues would have been significantly different. The new cast of characters were not so fortunate when the next crisis arose. What critical changes existed in 1860 that made the nature of the Civil War different? Which significant leaders were present in 1860 who would not have been significant in 1850? Do accidents of time, place, and circumstances often have a major influence on the outcome of events?

PRACTICE TEST

To help you evaluate your understanding of the lesson, turn to Appendix B and complete the Practice Test for the lesson. The Practice Test contains multiple choice questions and essay questions, followed by a Feedback Report with correct answers and references.

Lesson 21

The Fitful Fifties

LESSON ASSIGNMENTS

Review the following assignments in order to schedule your time appropriately. Pay careful attention; the titles and numbers of the textbook chapter, the telecourse guide lesson, and the video program may be different from one another.

Text: Nash, et al., *The American People, Volume One: To 1877,* Chapter 14, "The Union in Peril," pp. 481-493.

Reader: *Perspectives on America, Volume I,* "The Nature of Southern Separatism," by Potter.

Video: "The Fitful Fifties," from the Series, *The American Adventure.*

OVERVIEW

The Kansas sites of violence during the 1850s provide a setting for investigating the aftermath of the passage of the Kansas-Nebraska Act. The political reactions include the rise of the Republican party, an assault on Senator Sumner, and a split in the Democratic party.

INTRODUCTION

The Compromise of 1850 provided only temporary relief for the political turbulence of the United States. Before renewed hostilities broke out, the Election of 1852 served to prove that people wanted to avoid the issues. That the people elected attractive, articulate, and incompetent Franklin Pierce president was evidence of

---

their desire to evade the issues. For the moment, the winds of controversy were calmed.

Then in 1854, quite unintentionally, the slavery issue exploded back into prominence. Senator Stephen Douglas introduced the Kansas-Nebraska Bill into the Congress. The bill organized the Kansas Territory, repealed the Missouri Compromise line, and opened Kansas to slavery. When it passed, the North was enraged. Old political bonds burst and new alliances were formed. The Whig party disintegrated. Two new parties vied to take its place. The Republican party was formed, appealing to anti-slave sentiment, and it developed a well-rounded platform attractive to the North and West. The other party was the American party. It appealed to the bias some people exhibited against immigrants. By the end of the 1850s, the Republican party had gained dominance.

The most dramatic implications of the Kansas-Nebraska Act were worked out in the Kansas territory. A complex interplay of forces brought violence to the area. The usual conflicts over land titles, county seats, and offices were complicated by the issue of slavery in the land. Both pro-slave and anti-slave forces from outside the area tried to influence the situation. Disagreements led to violence and violence to a state of frontier war. The pro-slave attack on the town of Lawrence was answered by John Brown's assassinations at Pottawatomie, and that was followed by the pro-slave raid on Osawatomie. Stability was needed, but it seemed far away.

In an attempt to end the turmoil, a constitutional convention was called to meet in Lecompton, Kansas. Most of the anti-slave counties were not represented. The Lecompton Constitution was sent to the United States Congress with a petition for the state to be admitted as a slave state. After considerable manipulation, Kansas was invited to join the Union. However, an open referendum was required by the English bill. With federal marshals patrolling the polls, the Constitution and slave statehood were overwhelmingly rejected in Kansas. The few slaves that had been in Kansas numbered only two by the census of 1860.

The violence and bloodshed were not restricted to the plains of Kansas. Even on the Senate floor, the angry passions of the time resulted in bloodshed. Senator Charles Sumner was attacked a few days after making a passionate speech against southern slaveholders, especially the absent Senator Andrew P. Butler. Congressman Preston Brooks, a kinsman of Butler's, beat Sumner with a cane. The dual attacks brought out the worst in the country. The sectional hostility vented itself as public opinion was fed a steady diet of hatred. The fitful fifties had not yet ended, and the temper of the times gave little prospect for a peaceful solution to the problems.

LEARNING OBJECTIVES

Upon completion of the lesson you should develop and be able to demonstrate an understanding of:

1. The political developments of the 1850s, including presidential leadership and political parties.
2. The impact of the Kansas-Nebraska Bill on the settlement of Kansas, political parties, and Congress.
3. The increasing incidence of violence in the 1850s.

KEY TERMS

Look for these items as you proceed through the lesson assignments. Be able to define them upon completion of this lesson.

People

David Atchison	John. C. Fremont
Preston Brooks	Franklin Pierce
Andrew Butler	Winfield Scott
Frederick Douglass	Charles Sumner
Millard Fillmore	William Walker

Places

Cuba	Osawatomie
Lecompton	Pottawatomic Creek
Kansas Territory	36° 30′
Nebraska Territory	Topeka

Events and Terms

bleeding Kansas	Massachusetts Emigrant Aid
"filibusters"	Society

Continued on next page

Free Soilers   Ostend Manifesto
Kansas-Nebraska Act   Know-Nothing (American) party

<u>Ideas</u>

popular sovereignty   nativism

TEXT FOCUS POINTS

The following focus points are designed to help you get the most from the text. Review them, then read the assignment. You may want to write notes to reinforce what you have learned.

Text: Nash et al., *The American People,* Chapter 14, pp. 481-493.

1. What were the characteristics of the Election of 1852? What factors weakened the political party structure from 1852 to 1854?
2. What was the Kansas-Nebraska Act? What were Stephen Douglas's motives for introducing it? How did the public react to it?
3. Why did America's expansion energy weaken the Democratic party?
4. What changes were taking place in the American political party structure? What resulted from these changes by 1856?
5. What were the competitive forces trying to control Kansas? How did the competition lead to two seats of government?
6. What incidents of violence marred the Kansas situation? What did this reveal about the national argument between pro-slave and anti-slave forces?
7. Analyze the map on page 490. Where are Topeka, Lecompton, Pottawatomie Creek, and Osawatomie?
8. What was the northern view and vision for the United States?
9. What was the southern perspective?

READER FOCUS POINTS

Reader: *Perspectives on America, Volume I*, "The Nature of Southern Separatism," by Potter.

1. Why did the South's regional and national loyalties become conflicting loyalties?
2. What were the factors of affinity making cohesion in the South? How did the glorification of the plantation life and the planters fit into this unity? What was the role of racial prejudice?
3. What was the real issue for southerners to choose between regional or national loyalty?
4. What was the role of northern anti-slave attacks?
5. The South had sure consensus on what two important points?

VIDEO FOCUS POINTS

The following focus points are designed to help you get the most from the video segment of this lesson. Review them, then watch the video. You may want to write notes to reinforce what you have learned.

Video: "The Fitful Fifties"

Synopsis: Addresses the divisive power and the implications of the Kansas-Nebraska Act.

1. Why did slavery become an issue during the settlement of Kansas?
2. How was the level of violence escalated by events at Lawrence, Pottawatomie, and Osawatomie?
3. How did Professor Kathryn Sklar explain the rising level of violence?
4. What was the Sumner-Brooks Affair? What was the nation's reaction to it?
5. How were American political parties changing because of the turmoil in the 1850s?
6. What was Professor Sklar's analysis of these changes?

OPTIONAL LEARNING ACTIVITY

Write a two-page paper about John Brown's activities in Kansas. How did he justify his actions? What is your analysis of the man?

SUGGESTED READINGS

Further readings can be found in the text on pages 502-503.

HISTORICAL PERSPECTIVE

Fallout from the Kansas-Nebraska Act included two significant changes. First, the settlement of Kansas became a virtual dress rehearsal for the Civil War. Strong opinions were backed by violent action. Revenge begat revenge. Second, was a clear turn toward violence and away from compromise. Why had the nation made such alterations? While no single answer suffices to fully explain the changes, the weak presidents and shifting congressional leadership certainly failed to provide stability. A recent victorious war seemed to promote the validity of confrontation. And, of course, the frontier mentality of direct action played a role. These ingredients combined to presage a Union in peril.

PRACTICE TEST

To help you evaluate your understanding of the lesson, turn to Appendix B and complete the Practice Test for the lesson. The Practice Test contains multiple-choice questions and essay questions, followed by a Feedback Report with correct answers and references.

Lesson 22

Crisis of Union

LESSON ASSIGNMENTS

Review the following assignments in order to schedule your time appropriately. Pay careful attention; the titles and numbers of the textbook chapter, the telecourse guide lesson, and the video program may be different from one another.

Text: Nash, et al., *The American People, Volume One: To 1877*, Chapter 14, "The Union in Peril," pp. 493-503.

Reader: *Perspectives on America, Volume I*, "How We Got Lincoln," by Andrews.

Video: "Crisis of Union," from the Series, *The American Adventure*.

OVERVIEW

From the Illinois home of Abraham Lincoln to the federal fort in Charleston Harbor, the march toward tragedy is traced. The ascent of Lincoln's political star, the descent of Douglas's political fortunes, and the consequences of the election of 1860 sealed the fate of the nation.

INTRODUCTION

The disintegration of the political fabric continued as the 1850s drew to a close. As crisis neared, a cast of new characters emerged from the tangled affairs. In the Illinois Senate race of 1858, the fate of two major figures in the coming drama was determined. Senator Stephen A. Douglas was seeking re-election and attempting to establish momentum for an 1860 presidential bid. Abraham Lincoln challenged him. These old political foes debated the implications of the Dred Scott decision and slavery in general. Lincoln promoted the right of all people to enjoy the fruits of their labor. He did so without appearing to be an extremist. Lincoln's political potential was enhanced. Douglas tried to bridge the Dred Scott decision and popular sovereignty in order to maintain an acceptable posture for both northern and southern Democrats. But he failed and his political fortunes declined.

The raid on Harpers Ferry by John Brown on October 16, 1859, caused northern and southern hatreds to spew forth again. Moderate voices were drowned out by shrill accusations. Brown was a martyr to many in the North but a dangerous devil to the South. Emotions were prepared for a fateful impasse.

The election of 1860 provided the catalyst for the political explosion. The Democratic party split. Douglas finally was nominated by northern Democrats at a second "national" convention in 1860. He campaigned vigorously against Lincoln but also against the southern Democrats' nominee, John. C. Breckinridge. The Republicans, on the third ballot, selected the moderate Abraham Lincoln. Realizing victory was within their grasp, the Republicans carefully constructed a platform appealing to their various northern and western constituents, but they had no southern base. The fearful mid-staters organized a fourth campaign under the name Constitutional Union party and nominated John Bell. The peculiar combination of votes and sectionalism resulted in an unusual victory. Lincoln received 1.8 million votes, carried every non-slave state except New Jersey (split with Douglas), and won the election with 180 electoral votes. Douglas's national campaign garnered him the second most popular votes, but only 12 electoral votes. The other two candidates won a combined 111 electoral votes.

How would the South react to the election? South Carolina spoke first and decisively. Within weeks a special convention announced South Carolina was withdrawing from the Union. In February 1861 Texas became the seventh state of the deep South to leave. President Buchanan did little to stop the tide of secession, but he did keep war from erupting.

Lincoln, little known and frequently misunderstood, assumed office in March. He met the Carolians' challenge and vowed to supply Fort Sumter in Charleston Harbor. Shore batteries fired. Lincoln called for troops to stop rebellion. The Confederates called for volunteers to protect their new country. War was at hand.

LEARNING OBJECTIVES

Upon completion of the lesson you should develop and be able to demonstrate an understanding of:

1. The importance and nature of the Dred Scott decision.
2. The significance of the Lincoln-Douglas debates for each man and the country.
3. The significance of John Brown's raid on Harpers Ferry.
4. The candidates and issues in the election of 1860 and why South Carolina decided to secede from the Union.
5. The people and events that led from secession to Civil War.

KEY TERMS

Look for these items as you proceed through the lesson assignments. Be able to define them upon completion of this lesson.

People

Major Robert Anderson
John Bell
John. C. Breckinridge
John Brown
James Buchanan
Frederick Douglass

Stephen Douglas
Abraham Lincoln
Dred Scott
William Seward
Chief Justice Roger Taney

Places

Fort Sumter

Harpers Ferry

Events and Terms

"black Republican"
Confederate States of America
Constitutional Union party

Dred Scott v. Sanford
Lecompton Constitution
Republican Platform, 1860

Continued on next page

Idea

Secession

TEXT FOCUS POINTS

The following focus points are designed to help you get the most from the text. Review them, then read the assignment. You may want to write notes to reinforce what you have learned.

Text: Nash et al., *The American People,* Chapter 14, pp. 493-503.

1. What was the Dred Scott decision? What made it controversial?
2. How was Stephen Douglas's political position in the North and South affected by his opposition to the Lecompton Constitution?
3. How did the Lincoln-Douglas debates come about? What impacts did they have on the candidates and national politics?
4. Why did John Brown raid Harpers Ferry? What did he hope to accomplish? What impact did it have on the North and South?
5. Who were the candidates and what were the issues and results of the election of 1860? What do the table on page 487 and the map on page 498 reveal about the election?
6. Why did South Carolina secede from the Union? What resulted from their withdrawal? Why did the Republicans believe these states would be back?
7. What was the problem for the Union of maintaining Fort Sumter? What was Lincoln's reaction to South Carolina's attack?

READER FOCUS POINTS

Reader: *Perspectives on America, Volume I,* "How We Got Lincoln," by Andrews.

1. Why had Lincoln's name been introduced into the presidential race and how had he furthered his nomination chances?

2. Why did the convention site benefit Lincoln's chances? How did his floor managers get him the nomination? What had his men promised in order to secure his nomination?
3. How did the Republicans and Lincoln manage his presidential campaign? Who were his opponents and what groups supported each?

VIDEO FOCUS POINTS

The following focus points are designed to help you get the most from the video segment of this lesson. Review them, then watch the video. You may want to write notes to reinforce what you have learned.

Video: "Crisis of Union"

Synopsis: Addresses the continuation of the division of public opinion over slavery, leading to unrealistic characterization of each other, resulting in a breakdown of communications.

1. What was the reason for the Lincoln-Douglas debates? What impacts did the debates have on the careers of Douglas and Lincoln?
2. According to Professor Kathryn Sklar, what was significant about Lincoln's position in the debates?
3. What happened in response to John Brown's raid on Harpers Ferry?
4. What happened to the political party structure on the eve of the 1860 election? What were the results of that election?
5. Professor Sklar identified what factors as bringing the country to the brink of war by Spring, 1861?

OPTIONAL LEARNING ACTIVITY

What drew individuals into the Civil War? Using several primary sources, discuss in a two-page paper the reasons men and women supported the Civil War. What reason(s) do you find most compelling?

SUGGESTED READINGS

Further readings can be found in the text on pages 502-503

HISTORICAL PERSPECTIVE

The causes of the Civil War are still debated. But at root, the differences stemmed from the effect slave labor had on southern culture. The two sides had different economic thrusts due to slave or free labor. Could the two societies have continued united under the same government, or does the likelihood of a major disruption seem overwhelming?

PRACTICE TEST

To help you evaluate your understanding of the lesson, turn to Appendix B and complete the Practice Test for the lesson. The Practice Test contains multiple-choice questions and essay questions, followed by a Feedback Report with correct answers and references.

Lesson 23

A Frightful Conflict

LESSON ASSIGNMENTS

Review the following assignments in order to schedule your time appropriately. Pay careful attention; the titles and numbers of the textbook chapter, the telecourse guide lesson, and the video program may be different from one another.

Text: Nash, et al., *The American People, Volume One: To 1877*, Chapter 15, "The Union Severed," pp. 504-529.

Reader: *Perspectives on America, Volume I*, "Prison Camps of the Civil War," by Catton.

Video: "A Frightful Conflict," from the Series, *The American Adventure*.

OVERVIEW

The tragic beauty of the Vicksburg and Gettysburg battle sites, Sherman's headquarters in Savannah, and the serene melancholy of Appomattox set the tone for analyzing both the military and the human dimensions of America's most significant war.

INTRODUCTION

The "preamble" was over and "the great and tragic volume" had begun. Lincoln's and Davis's initial calls for troops were met enthusiastically. The sparring ended soon enough, and the bloodiest war in American history began. The Union and Confederate forces seemed poorly matched. The North had overwhelming superiority in population, industrial production, railroads, and natural resources. But, with interior lines of defense and superior general officers, the South made northern victory painfully difficult.

The military issues revolved around strategy and leadership. The Confederacy chose to maintain a defensive posture, with occasional offensive thrusts to weaken northern resolve. The North eventually decided on a three-part strategic plan. One element was to divide the South along the Mississippi River, effectively dividing it in half. A second was to blockade the Confederate coastline to stop both exports and needed imports. A third was to capture the Confederate capital, which had been moved to Richmond, Virginia, tantalizingly close to Washington, D.C. In order to accomplish these goals, the North used an exhaustion strategy in the western theater and an annihilation strategy in the eastern theater. But not until Grant adopted Lincoln's policy of simultaneous advances was the war ended.

The battles were frequent, vicious, and costly. But the momentum was decisively altered at three sites. In September 1862, the Union stopped Lee's northward thrust at Antietam Creek, Maryland. Although the Union missed an opportunity for a crushing victory, Lincoln used that moment to announce his intention to free all Confederate slaves on January 1, 1863, if the rebellion continued. In that way, the push of Union military force would undo the South's peculiar institution. The Emancipation Proclamation did not free slaves in the Union States, but if the overwhelming majority of slaves were freed, the others could not be ignored. For many Europeans, this additional Union goal made support for the South impossible.

Propaganda aside, the war still had to be won on the battlefield. The pivotal moments came in July 1863 when simultaneous Union victories all but sealed the Confederacy's fate. Along the Mississippi River, the forces maneuvered for control. Vicksburg became the focal point. The Union Army was commanded by General Ulysses S. Grant. After a six-week siege, he drew the defenders of the city into a fight. With daring and resourcefulness, Grant captured the defending army and the civilians at Vicksburg. A few days later, miles downriver, Port Hudson fell and the Union had the grand old river. Meanwhile, Robert E. Lee had plunged ahead with a gambler's boldness. His efforts brought an irreversible loss at Gettysburg. Unable to win his objective, a decisive victory on Union soil, Lee limped back to his defense of Richmond. The end did not come quickly or easily, but the South never again had the winner's momentum.

As the war continued, southern resources and lands were devastated. In the fall of 1864, Atlanta, Georgia, was taken by General William T. Sherman. President

Lincoln's bid for reelection was rejuvenated by the news, and the South's fate was merely a matter of time and place. The end came when Lee surrendered to the ever-pressing army of Grant at Appomattox Courthouse, Virginia. The fighting lingered sporadically for a few more weeks, but the great southern armies were gone. The most costly war in American history was finished, its legacies yet unknown.

LEARNING OBJECTIVES

Upon completion of the lesson you should develop and be able to demonstrate an understanding of:

1. The creation, organization, and deployment of the Confederate and Union forces.
2. The ebb and flow of the military fate of the two sides from Bull Run to Appomattox Courthouse.
3. The political and military leadership of the two sides.
4. The nature of the defeat suffered by the Confederacy.

KEY TERMS

Look for these items as you proceed through the lesson assignments. Be able to define them upon completion of this lesson.

People

Arthur Carpenter
George Eagleton
General Ulysses S. Grant
Horace Greeley
Henri Jomini

General Robert E. Lee
Abraham Lincoln
General George McClellan
William Seward

Places

Battle of Antietam

Battle of Shiloh Church

Continued on next page

Battle of Bull Run   Battle of Vicksburg
Battle of Chancellorsville   Savannah
Battle of Gettysburg

Events and Terms

The Alabama   *Ex Parte Merryman*
Border States   greenbacks
bounties   ironclads
draft   *Merrimac*
Emancipation Proclamation   *Monitor*

Ideas

blockade   emancipation

TEXT FOCUS POINTS

The following focus points are designed to help you get the most from the text. Review them, then read the assignment. You may want to write notes to reinforce what you have learned.

Text: Nash et al., *The American People,* Chapter 15, pp. 504-529.

1. What were the initial reactions to the bombardment of Fort Sumter? Lincoln's call for troops? (Use the table on page 496 to help with the answer.)
2. What was the comparative balance of resources for the Union and Confederacy as the war began?
3. Use the màp on page 509 to answer these questions. What were the first seven states to secede from the Union? Which of the remaining eight seceded? Which slave states remained in the Union?
4. How did the "border" states react to the crisis?

5. How did the Confederacy and Jefferson Davis organize the southern government? Lincoln his? How did the two compare?
6. What were the major military events of 1861-1862 in the eastern theater? The western theater?
7. Locate on the map on page 513 the battles of Antietam and Bull Run. Where is Richmond, Virginia?
8. Analyze the map on page 514. Where are Fort Donelson, Fort Henry, Shiloh, Vicksburg, and Port Hudson?
9. What role did the Union and the Confederate navies play in the war?
10. What were the comparative diplomatic policies of the Union and Confederacy?
11. What solutions were found to problems of manpower and finances for both sides?
12. What elements of political dissension arose on the home fronts?
13. What was the Emancipation Proclamation? What impact did it have on the war?
14. What were some unexpected consequences of the war?
15. On the map on page 524 find Gettysburg, Chancellorsville, Appomattox Courthouse, Atlanta, and Savannah.
16. What was the progression of military events from Chancellorsville to Savannah? What were Lee's, Grant's, and Sherman's roles in those events?

READER FOCUS POINTS

Reader: *Perspectives on America, Volume I*, "Prison Camps of the Civil War," by Catton.

1. What was the real cause of the horrors of Andersonville Prison?
2. Why did the old exchange system break down?
3. What problems did Wirz face at Andersonville?
4. Why were the prison camps such a problem? How were prisons in the North?

VIDEO FOCUS POINTS

The following focus points are designed to help you get the most from the video segment of this lesson. Review them, then watch the video. You may want to write notes to reinforce what you have learned.

Video: "A Frightful Conflict"

Synopsis: Addresses the organization of the great armies and the impact of war on the generals, common soldiers, and civilians.

1. What were the peculiar horrors of the Civil War?
2. How did Professor Peter Maslowski explain the duration of the Civil War? What were each side's advantages and disadvantages?
3. What was the significance of Antietam?
4. Why was the war basically decided in July 1863?
5. What was General William T. Sherman's attitude toward winning the war?
6. What was Professor Maslowski's analysis of the Union victory?

OPTIONAL LEARNING ACTIVITIES

1. Write a two-page paper analyzing the pros and cons of Sherman's March to the Sea. What were the impacts of his tactics on the South? The North?
2. Write a two-page paper based on the article in the textbook on pages 526-527. (Note: Video Lesson 23 has some additional Brady photographs.)

SUGGESTED READINGS

Further readings can be found in the text on page 537.

HISTORICAL PERSPECTIVE

The Civil War remains the most dramatic single episode in American history. It seems to hold a kind of morbid fascination. It was also a watershed in American history. Not only was slavery destroyed in its wake, so was the young nation's innocence. The industrial and financial resources of the country entered a new phase of development. Most amazing of all, within a few decades the whole country took pride in how the political fabric of the United States had survived the great task. What other results of the war are most striking? Could they have been accomplished without the tumult of war?

PRACTICE TEST

To help you evaluate your understanding of the lesson, turn to Appendix B and complete the Practice Test for the lesson. The Practice Test contains multiple-choice questions and essay questions, followed by a Feedback Report with correct answers and references.

Lesson 24

The Home Fronts

LESSON ASSIGNMENTS

Review the following assignments in order to schedule your time appropriately. Pay careful attention; the titles and numbers of the textbook chapter, the telecourse guide lesson, and the video program may be different from one another.

Text: Nash, et al., *The American People, Volume One: To 1877*, Chapter 15, "The Union Severed," pp. 529-537.

Video: "The Home Fronts," from the Series, *The American Adventure*.

OVERVIEW

The devastated fields and cities of the South are contrasted with the prosperity of the North. The political and economic events of the Union and Confederacy provide a dual view of the social and economic impact of the Civil War—a tragedy compounded by the assassination at Ford's Theater.

INTRODUCTION

The Civil War impacted America far beyond the horrible casualty lists and military events. It had the character of total war which strained at the economic, social, and political fabric of both sides. The long-term economic advantages of the Union were not apparent in the first year of the war. The North struggled to get its clothing, munitions, merchant marine, and steel industries into war production. The Confederacy managed to import or manufacture most of their necessities until the late stages of the war. The North's financial resources held up much better than the

South's, and by 1863 was fueling a real prosperity for many Americans. The general health of the Union's economy was substantial, while the South's financial resources quickly eroded. By war's end, personal privations and economic ruin stalked the Confederacy and the distribution of goods came to a standstill. While crops rotted in the fields and railroad stations, troops went without and civilians starved. Although not all northerners prospered, many did and overall production was up. Not all southerners went without, but tens of thousands did and the economy was wrecked by war's end.

The social-political stability of both sides was tested by the war. As the war went badly for the Confederacy, the political and social unity of secession crumbled. The nonslaveholders began to question why they were fighting while many of the rich were exempted. Frequently slaves fled to the Union. State political leaders questioned the military and civilian heads of the Confederacy as losing bred distrust, hatred, and contempt.

Likewise, the Union suffered social and political stress. The draft set off protests from the lower class and immigrants, which sometimes reached severe proportions. Conspicuous consumption by the upper class, especially in urban areas, caused considerable unrest among the laboring classes who struggled to make a living. In the political arena, friction continued between Lincoln and his Democratic opponents. The president frequently used extraordinary executive measures to try to control dissension. He used drastic means to accomplish political goals. The president was also confronted by more radical members of his own Republican party over issues of reconstructing governmental authority in the southern states. Political disagreements were so great in the Union that Lincoln thought as late as September 1864 that he might not win reelection. But thanks in part to Sherman's conquest of Atlanta, he was reelected.

Left in the war's wake were bitter legacies. A devastated southern home front was a constant reminder of death and loss. Confederates recognized defeat but wanted desperately to regain control of their lands and destiny. The North had the difficult task of finding a balance between vindictive punishment and reasonable realignment of states within the Union. Perhaps the most tragic of all the war's legacies was the brutal silencing of the most powerful voice of moderation by an assassin's bullet in Ford's Theater. With Lincoln's death, peaceful reconstruction was a faint hope.

LEARNING OBJECTIVES

Upon completion of the lesson you should develop and be able to demonstrate an understanding of:

1. The economic impact of the Civil War on the North and the South.
2. The political problems behind both Union and Confederate lines.
3. The legacies of the Civil War.
4. The significance of Lincoln's assassination and its implications for Reconstruction.

KEY TERMS

Look for these items as you proceed through the lesson assignments. Be able to define them upon completion of this lesson.

People

Clara Barton
Elizabeth Blackwell
Emily Blackwell
Jefferson Davis
Sherman
Dorothea Dix

Emily Harris
Abraham Lincoln
General George McClellan
General William Tecumseh

Places

Appomattox Courthouse

Ford's Theater

Events and Terms

Blockade
Conscription Acts
Homestead Act, 1862

McCormick reaper
Morrill Act, 1862
Pacific Railroad Act, 1862

Ideas

inflation

shortages

TEXT FOCUS POINTS

The following focus points are designed to help you get the most from the text. Review them, then read the assignment. You may want to write notes to reinforce what you have learned.

Text: Nash et al., *The American People,* Chapter 15, pp. 529-537.

1. What were Confederate leaders forced to do with governmental power in order to try to win the war?
2. What changes occurred in southern agriculture and class structure?
3. What more permanent changes took place in northern financial and economic affairs?
4. What social changes came with the war?
5. What impact did the war have on blacks and women?
6. How and why did Lincoln win reelection in 1864?
7. Why did the North win the war?
8. What were the economic and human costs of the war?
9. What questions lingered as the war ended? How did Lincoln's assassination compound the difficulties?

VIDEO FOCUS POINTS

The following focus points are designed to help you get the most from the video segment of this lesson. Review them, then watch the video. You may want to write notes to reinforce what you have learned.

Video: "The Home Fronts"

Synopsis: Addresses the contrasts and comparisons in social, political, and economic impacts of the Civil War on the Union and Confederacy.

1. What fears did the later years of the war bring to the southern home front?
2. What was Professor Harvey Graff's characterization of the economic impact of the Civil War on the North? The South?

---

3. What impact did the Civil War have on slavery, according to Professor Eric Foner?
4. What appeared to be Lincoln's attitude toward reconstruction?
5. What did Professor Foner say was the impact of Lincoln's death on the prospects for reunion?

OPTIONAL LEARNING ACTIVITY

After reading some personal accounts of life during the Civil War, write your own two page, first-person account of life during the war. Feel free to use your imagination, but be as realistic and sensitive as possible to the circumstances.

SUGGESTED READINGS

Further readings can be found in the text on page 537.

HISTORICAL PERSPECTIVE

That the country survived the trauma of the Civil War with its primary economic, social, and political institutions intact is amazing. Frequently, such an emotional and divisive event destroys some of those basic ideals. Why did the United States retain its institutional integrity? Once slavery was ended, had the major difference between unionists and confederates been eliminated? What were the most lasting elements of division that remained? Could the United States have obtained its present world status if slavery had remained? If the South had remained independent? Considering these factors, what do you believe were the most notable results of the Civil War period for the United States?

PRACTICE TEST

To help you evaluate your understanding of the lesson, turn to Appendix B and complete the Practice Test for the lesson. The Practice Test contains multiple-choice questions and essay questions, followed by a Feedback Report with correct answers and references.

Lesson 25

Reconstructing the South

LESSON ASSIGNMENTS

Review the following assignments in order to schedule your time appropriately. Pay careful attention; the titles and numbers of the textbook chapter, the telecourse guide lesson, and the video program may be different from one another.

Text: Nash, et al., *The American People, Volume One: To 1877*, Chapter 16, "The Union Reconstructed," pp. 538-553.

Reader: *Perspectives on America, Volume I*, "The New View of Reconstruction," by Foner.

Video: "Reconstructuring the South," from the Series, *The American Adventure*.

OVERVIEW

A ruined plantation, a Union-Confederate boundary, and the capital city symbolize the traumas and pains of reunion. The difficult social, economic, and political adjustments in the aftermath of Civil War are highlighted in a discussion of the period of Reconstruction.

INTRODUCTION

The war was over, but the hating would not be stopped so quickly. Four years of killing, sacrificing, and agonizing would only be forgotten with time. But some things would not wait. What would happen to the former slaves? How would government be established in the South? Who would control those governments?

How would the national economy be rebuilt? These questions and a myriad of others had to be dealt with in the years immediately following the war.

The task of binding the country's wounds fell to a southern Democrat-Unionist named Andrew Johnson. Although chosen by the Republican-Union party leaders, he was not expected to become president. But John Wilkes Booth's actions thrust him into the office. Johnson's public statements indicated a more intransigent stand than Lincoln's, and for that some radicals in Congress were grateful. Johnson went ahead with a plan for reunion of the Confederate states that was very much like Lincoln's. Under Johnson's plan southerners who took loyalty oaths, with a few exceptions that included the wealthiest Confederates, could create new state governments. By the time Congress assembled in December 1865, all eleven states had written new constitutions, elected state officials, and selected new Senators and Representatives, but reconstruction was not to be accomplished so easily.

With good reason, many in the Congress doubted the loyalty and sincerity of southerners. Despite Johnson's restrictions, many of the officials in the new governments had been Confederate leaders. Many were granted special pardons by the president. The state governments also passed new laws called the black codes, which defined the freed slaves' roles in very limited terms. The Congress, led by a vocal group of radical Republicans, began to move. An act extending the Freedmen's Bureau passed in February. This wartime agency was created to help the former slaves. A Civil Rights bill passed in March. Johnson not only vetoed both, but he also raised the level of rhetoric to new heights of rancor.

The first Congressional reconstruction plan was imbedded in the Fourteenth Amendment. Johnson advised the states to reject it, and ten of the eleven ex-Confederate states did. Only his home state, Tennessee, accepted it. Congress then passed the Freedmen's Bureau and Civil Rights Act over Johnson's vetoes. The Congressional election of 1866 became pivotal. The president campaigned vigorously against many Republicans. Most of the candidates he supported lost, and Congress came more under the dominance of radicals.

In spring 1867, Congress passed a new and final Reconstruction Plan. It was much more demanding on the South. The ten states that did not accept the Fourteenth Amendment (Tennessee's government had been recognized and their Congressional delegation seated) were divided into five military districts. The commanding general was to oversee the creation of new state governments and to enroll all eligible voters — including all black males twenty-one-years of age or older. The act also required each new government to ratify the Fourteenth Amendment before it would be formally allowed to send delegates to Congress.

These radical governments depended on a fragile alliance of carpetbaggers, northerners who had come south to participate in remaking the region; scalawags, white southerners who were willing to cooperate with the radicals; and the freedmen. Obviously, black votes were necessary to keep the coalition together. Thus, Congress passed the Fifteenth Amendment which barred the use of race as a barrier to voting. President Johnson fought the radicals every step. Finally, he defied the Tenure of Office Act by removing Secretary of War Edwin Stanton. The House hastily impeached the president. The Senate narrowly failed to convict him. The turmoil of establishing a reconstruction policy bode ill for the prospects of implementing one.

LEARNING OBJECTIVES

Upon completion of the lesson you should develop and be able to demonstrate an understanding of:

1. The difficulties of overcoming the hostilities left by the Civil War and reuniting the country.
2. The role and place of freedmen in the post Civil War South.
3. The role of Andrew Johnson in Reconstruction politics and why he was impeached.
4. The nature of the military reconstruction plans of Congress.
5. The significance of the Thirteenth, Fourteenth, and Fifteenth Amendments.

KEY TERMS

Look for these items as you proceed through the lesson assignments. Be able to define them upon completion of this lesson.

People

Adele Allston   Edwin Stanton
Elizabeth Allston   Elizabeth Cady Stanton
Susan B. Anthony   Thaddeus Stevens
Andrew Johnson   Charles Sumner

Places

Memphis   New Orleans

Events and Terms

black codes   Freedmen's Bureau
"bloody shirt" campaigning   impeachment
Civil Rights Bill   Joint Committee on Reconstruction
Fifteenth Amendment   Southern Homestead Act, 1866
40 acres and a mule   Tenure of Office Act
Fourteenth Amendment   Thirteenth Amendment
freedmen

Idea

"Africanized"

TEXT FOCUS POINTS

The following focus points are designed to help you get the most from the text. Review them, then read the assignment. You may want to write notes to reinforce what you have learned.

Text: Nash et al., *The American People,* Chapter 16, pp. 538-553.

1. What were the different attitudes of the president and Congress over which agency of government should oversee reconstruction?
2. What were the economic conditions of the North and South at war's end?
3. How did the freedmen react to their new status?
4. What were the immediate responses of white southerners to the changes? What were the "black codes"?
5. What was Andrew Johnson's plan for Reconstruction? How successful was it?
6. Why did Congress reject Johnson's plans?
7. What was the Congressional plan of reconstruction?
8. Why did the Congress impeach Andrew Johnson? What actions followed his impeachment?
9. In what ways were the actions of Congress moderate in the Reconstruction Era? What were the reconstruction amendments? Why did they upset many women?

READER FOCUS POINTS

Reader: *Perspectives on America, Volume I,* "The New View of Reconstruction," by Foner.

1. What was the common view of Reconstruction before 1960?
2. What were the revised opinions of the radicals? The new assessment of events and groups in the South during Reconstruction?
3. What have new investigations revealed about the transition from slavery to freedom?

---

4. What helps to explain the ferocity of the attacks on Reconstruction participants? How does the immediate outcome of Reconstruction underscore its uniqueness?

VIDEO FOCUS POINTS

The following focus points are designed to help you get the most from the video segment of this lesson. Review them, then watch the video. You may want to write notes to reinforce what you have learned.

Video: "Reconstructing the South"

Synopsis: Addresses the evolvement of radical control of reconstruction and its impact on national politics.

1. What were the elements of the invisible wall separating Union and ex-Confederate states?
2. What was Andrew Johnson's political and social background?
3. How did Professor Eric Foner explain the confrontation over Reconstruction between Andrew Johnson and Congressional leaders?
4. What factors helped the radicals gain control of Reconstruction?
5. According to Professor Foner, why did Johnson's Reconstruction program fail? What were the goals of radical reconstruction?

OPTIONAL LEARNING ACTIVITY

You are the attorney for Andrew Johnson in his impeachment trial. Write a two-page brief (outline) of the defense strategy you would follow. What do you believe is your strongest point?

SUGGESTED READINGS

Further readings can be found in the text on pages 572-573.

HISTORICAL PERSPECTIVE

The radicals' success in reconstructing the South hinged on the support of almost all freedmen and a few white southerners. Black support depended on maintaining the necessary climate of political, social, and economic rights. The resolve to continue support for these policies finally dissolved and traditional political leadership reemerged in the old Confederacy. What would have happened if black constitutional protections had been enforced by law and supported by economic opportunity? Could the civil and political rights turmoils of the 1960s and 1970s have been worked out a hundred years earlier? The latter we will never know, but the great controversies over equal rights have a long and checkered history.

PRACTICE TEST

To help you evaluate your understanding of the lesson, turn to Appendix B and complete the Practice Test for the lesson. The Practice Test contains multiple-choice questions and essay questions, followed by a Feedback Report with correct answers and references.

Lesson 26

The End of an Era

LESSON ASSIGNMENTS

Review the following assignments in order to schedule your time appropriately. Pay careful attention; the titles and numbers of the textbook chapter, the telecourse guide lesson, and the video program may be different from one another.

Text: Nash et al., *The American* People, Chapter 16, pp. 553-572.

Video: "The End of an Era,"
          from the series, *The American Adventure*.

OVERVIEW

Washington, D.C., and Selma, Alabama, represent the successes, failures, and incompleteness of Reconstruction events. The course ends with a look backward and forward, from America's centennial celebration in 1876, to catch a glimpse of the future of the United States in its second century.

INTRODUCTION

The establishment of Congressional Reconstruction policies not only divided northern public opinion, but their implementation caused violence and pain for the many participants in the South. The governments created by the constitutional conventions in each of the ten former Confederate states (all except Tennessee) brought to power a coalition of three groups. The carpetbaggers, northern men who came South to be involved in remaking the states, provided leadership and sometimes ties to federal authorities. They varied significantly in quality and motivation. Southern white men who supported these governments were called scalawags. Frequently, they were pre-war Unionists from the small farmer class and a few wealthy former Whig politicians. But the most critical element of the coalition was the freedmen. The black men had to provide the votes to carry out radical policies and control state offices. These radical plans demanded cooperation and consensus among all three elements. The level of cooperation soon broke down and all the hopes for a Republican South, and black equality and opportunity were lost.

The opposition to radical governments came from the pre-war Democratic leadership. Had northern leaders been willing to continue the fight for a "new South" the results might have been different. But the North lost interest. With the Depression of 1873, more pressing matters pushed Reconstruction from center stage. All exconfederates were pardoned by 1873. The southern Democrats regained control of one state after another by the use of racism, intimidation, and prejudice. Such organizations as the Ku Klux Klan and the red shirts effectively divided southern Republicans. Once in control, the Democratic administrations diminished the role and opportunities for blacks. Although blacks made some gains, what might have been a triumph in American racial relations was lost and the issues left for later generations of Americans to settle.

The last of the radical governments was undermined as a result of the presidential election of 1876. The electoral results seemed to elect a Democrat, Samuel Tilden, but twenty disputed electoral votes changed the winner. Nineteen of the votes came from the three remaining Republican controlled southern states. An electoral commission decided all twenty votes (one from Oregon) should be awarded to Rutherford. B. Hayes, but in order to get a filibuster ended in the Senate, a compromise was needed. Among the things Hayes agreed to do was remove troops from the South. The removal of the troops from Louisiana, South Carolina, and Florida resulted in them being "redeemed" into the Democratic party. The "new South" was, once again, solidly Democratic.

So, as the United States ended its first century of independence, the trauma of Civil War was slowly mending. Although the social and political agenda was retarded, the economic possibilities burst forth with renewed vigor. The country was poised at a critical juncture between the agrarian, expansive past and the crowded, industrial future. The American Adventure would require a new perspective.

LEARNING OBJECTIVES

Upon completion of the lesson you should develop and be able to demonstrate an understanding of:

1. The participants in radical Reconstruction and the impact of Reconstruction on the South.
2. The reasons the northern Republicans lost interest in Reconstruction.
3. The significance and role of violent organizations in the ending of radical Reconstruction.
4. The role of the freedmen in Reconstruction and what happened to them with the end of radical Reconstruction.
5. How the election of 1876 led to the last withdrawal of Federal troops from the South.

KEY TERMS

Look for these items as you proceed through the lesson assignments. Be able to define them upon completion of this lesson.

People

Henry Adams	Andrew Johnson
Horace Greeley	Ku Klux Klan (KKK)
Ulysses S. Grant	Benjamin "Pap" Singleton
Rutherford B. Hayes	Samuel J. Tilden

Place

Selma Bridge

Events and Terms

African Methodist Episcopal Church	Freedmen's Bureau
Mississippi Plan	carpetbaggers

Continued on next page

New York Tribune Compromise of 1877
Republican coalition Crédit Mobilier
redemption (redeemers) debt peonage
sharecroppers Election of 1876
tenancy Force Acts
Tweed Ring

TEXT FOCUS POINTS

The following focus points are designed to help you get the most from the text. Review them, then read the assignment. You may want to write notes to reinforce what you have learned.

Text: Nash et al., *The American* People, Chapter 16, pp. 553-572.

1. What was the purpose and role of the Freedmen's Bureau? What were its successes and failures?
2. What caused a new economic dependency for the freedmen? What resulted from this change?
3. What do the maps on page 556 reveal about black freedmen after Reconstruction?
4. What institutions did blacks develop to help themselves adjust to the new situation?
5. What were the misconceptions about congressional Reconstruction governments? What was the reality of these governments?
6. What were the three main groups of supporters for radical governments?
7. How were the radical governments expelled from office? What happened following their expulsion?
8. Analyze the map on page 562 When had all the Confederate states returned to full Union membership? How long did Republicans retain control in each state?

9. Why did northerners allow the abuses in removing the Reconstruction governments? What were the characteristics of Grant and the national scene in the late 1860s and 1870s?
10. What brought about the end of radical Reconstruction governments?

VIDEO FOCUS POINTS

The following focus points are designed to help you get the most from the video segment of this lesson. Review them, then watch the video. You may want to write notes to reinforce what you have learned.

Video: "The End of An Era"

Synopsis: Addresses the reganing of political dominance by white southern Democrats from radical reconstructionists.

1. What had many blacks been forced to do following emancipation in order to work?
2. What was the actual role of blacks in the Reconstruction process?
3. What problems of the freedmen did Professor Alphine Jefferson discuss?
4. What was the contrast between dream and reality for the freedmen?
5. According to Professor Foner, why did southern white Democrats regain rule of the state governments?
6. What were the legacies of the American Adventure for the second century of United States history?

OPTIONAL LEARNING ACTIVITY

Combine the information from the dramatic illustrated material in Program 26 and the excerpts from Tourgee and Dixon on page 567, and write a two-page paper comparing and contrasting the various views of the freedmen and klansmen during Reconstruction.

HISTORICAL PERSPECTIVE

The disputed election of 1876 is a fascinating event in the history of the United States. Students of the period believe that Tilden probably should have won, but corruption and intimidation was rampant on both sides. The Compromise of 1877 was successful because southern Democratic Senators voted to stop the filibusters and count the electoral vote. Southern Senators seemed less concerned with which northern man would be president than getting the last of the federal troops out of the South. Who were the real winners from the final settlement? Who were the biggest losers? Could such an electoral impasse happen again? Why or why not?

PRACTICE TEST

To help you evaluate your understanding of the lesson, turn to Appendix B and complete the Practice Test for the lesson. The Practice Test contains multiple-choice questions and essay questions, followed by a Feedback Report with correct answers and references.

Appendix A—Contributors

We gratefully acknowledge the valuable contributions to this course from the following individuals. Their titles were accurate when the video programs were recorded, but may have changed since the original taping.

Lesson 1 — "Consequences of Contact"

Professor Gary Nash, University of California-Los Angeles

Lesson 2 — "English Colonization of the Chesapeake"

Professor Edmund Morgan, Yale University

Lesson 3 — "A Puritan Way"

Professor Edmund Morgan, Yale University

Lesson 4 — "Diversification of the Colonies"

Professor Gary Nash, University of California—Los Angeles

Lesson 5 — "The Colonial Experience"

Professor Gary Nash, University of California—Los Angeles
Professor Edmund Morgan, Yale University

Lesson 6 — "A New Society"

Professor John A. Trickel, Richland College

Lesson 7 — "Struggle for Dominance"

Professor Edmund Morgan, Yale University

Lesson 8 — "A Revolution for Independence"

Professor Peter Maslowski, University of Nebraska-Lincoln

Lesson 9 — "The Problems of Confederation"

Professor Forrest McDonald, University of Alabama

Lesson 10 — "Creating a Stronger Union"

Professor Forrest McDonald, University of Alabama

Lesson 11 — "The Republic in a Hostile World"

Professor Forrest McDonald, University of Alabama

Lesson 12 — "The Rural Republic"

Professor Julie Roy Jeffrey, Goucher College

Lesson 13 — "The Failure of Diplomacy"

Professor Peter Maslowski, University of Nebraska-Lincoln

Contributors
204

Lesson 14 — "Good Feelings and Bad"

Professor K. Jack Bauer, Rensselaer Polytechnic Institute

Lesson 15 — "The Expanding Nation"

Professor Julie Jeffrey, Goucher College
Professor R. David Edmunds, Texas Christian University

Lesson 16 — "The South's Slave System"

Professor Alphine Jefferson, Southern Methodist University

Lesson 17 — "The Jacksonian Persuasion"

Professor Edward Pessen, Baruch College, and the Graduate School of the City University of New York.

Lesson 18 — "Reforming the Republic"

Professor Harvey Graff, University of Texas-Dallas

Lesson 19 — "Manifest Destiny"

Professor K. Jack Bauer, Rensselaer Polytechnic Institute

Lesson 20 — "Agitation and Compromise"

Professor Eric Foner, Columbia University

Lesson 21 — "The Fitful Fifties"

Professor Kathryn Kish Sklar, University of California-Los Angeles

Lesson 22 — "Crisis of Union"

Professor Kathryn Kish Sklar, University of California-Los Angeles

Lesson 23 — "A Frightful Conflict"

Professor Peter Maslowski, University of Nebraska-Lincoln

Lesson 24 — "The Home Fronts"

Professor Harvey Graff, University of Texas at Dallas Professor Eric Foner, Columbia University

Lesson 25 — "Reconstructuring the South"

Professor Eric Foner, Columbia University

Lesson 26 — "The End of an Era"

Professor Alphine Jefferson, Southern Methodist University
Professor Eric Foner, Columbia University

Appendix B–Practice Tests

The following practice tests contain multiple-choice and essay questions for each of the twenty-six lessons. Many questions require straight, factual answers while others call for interpretation or application of information.

Practice Test Organization

The Practice Test for any lesson can be identified by referring to the footer at the bottom of the page which includes the lesson number, the title of the lesson, and the page numbers.

The practice tests for the lessons are ordered consecutively, so that Lesson 1 is first, followed by Lesson 2, and so on. Each lesson has its own separate practice tests of multiple-choice and essay questions.

Feedback Report Explanation

The feedback reports include the correct answers for multiple-choice questions and reference information to the material addressed by the question.

The reference indicates the learning objectives (Obj) and applicable page numbers of the material addressed by the questions.

Example

Ref: (Obj. 1, pp. 136-138, Video) indicates that the question relates to:

- Learning Objective 1
- Pages 136-138 in the textbook
- Also relates to the video program

Multiple-Choice

Select the single best answer. If more than one answer is required, it will be so indicated.

1. As the Europeans began to arrive in the 1500s in the New World, they found
    A. inhabitants who had common societal forms throughout the region.
    B. inhabitants whose societies were similar to their own.
    C. inhabitants who had maintained the same lifestyle for 15,000 years.
    — D. inhabitants with complex and unique societies.

2. According to the Native American world view,
    A. the Europeans were welcomed to their lands.
    B. no foreign groups could enter tribal lands.
    C. there was individual ownership of land.
    — D. each tribe held communal ownership of the land.

3. When the Europeans first encountered sub-Sahara Africa, they found a
    A. backward region of primitive tribes.
    B. region that had remained isolated from the rest of the world.
    C. region more advanced than their own.
    D. region as complex as their own.

4. The greatest impact of Portuguese exploration was
    A. introducing Europe to the potential that could be achieved through trade.
    B. mapping important water routes to the Western Hemisphere.
    C. Prince Henry's role in European diplomacy.
    D. finding a passage to the Australian continent.

5. Professor Gary Nash stated in the video program that one of the most important results of European and native contact was the introduction of certain crops to the European diet. What were they?
   A. Wheat, rye, and barley
   — B. Potatoes, beans, and corn
   C. Wheat, corn, and oats
   D. Potatoes, rye, and oats

6. The rise of the monarchs in Europe meant
   A. widespread revolutions.
   — B. order and stability.
   C. economic reversals.
   D. population decline and civil disobedience.

7. By the end of the sixteenth century, Spain
   — A. was the most powerful nation in Europe.
   B. was forced to admit her voyages had been a failure.
   C. was the dominant power in Africa.
   D. began to explore for new routes to the East.

8. The Spanish conquest of the Aztec society was made easier by
   A. the superior numbers of Spanish soldiers.
   B. the lack of enthusiasm by the Aztec warriors.
   C. Montezuma's inspiring leadership.
   — D. the hostility of many native tribes toward the Aztecs.

9. The greatest loss of life for Native Americans during the sixteenth and seventeenth centuries was caused by
   A. intertribal warfare.
   B. intermarriage with Europeans.
   C. conversion to European religions.
   — D. infectious diseases brought by Europeans.

Essay Questions

10. The Europeans arrived in the New World with the preconceived notion that native groups were heathens and barbarians. How correct was this assumption? Support your answer with specific examples of the types of native cultures which had developed by the fifteenth century.

11. Discuss the factors that contributed to Spanish and Portuguese exploration and colonization of the New World in the fifteenth and sixteenth centuries. What did each of these factors contribute to this exploration-colonization impulse? Explain.

12. The consequences of contact between Europeans and Native Americans were profound and enduring. Explain the significance of the exchange of foods, animals, and diseases. Which factor had the greatest impact on the Native tribes? The Europeans? Why?

FEEDBACK REPORT

1. D   Ref: (obj. 1, pp. 6-7)
2. D   Ref: (obj. 1, pp. 9, 13)
3. D   Ref: (obj. 1, pp. 14-15)
4. A   Ref: (obj. 2, pp. 18-19, Video)
5. B   Ref: (obj. 3, Video, Nash interview #3)
6. B   Ref: (obj. 1, p. 18)
7. A   Ref: (obj. 2, pp. 23-24, Video)
8. D   Ref: (obj. 2, p. 24, Video, Reader Article for Lesson 1)
9. D   Ref: (obj. 3, pp. 25-26, Video, Nash interview #1)
10.   Ref: (obj. 1, pp. 23-26)
11.   Ref: (obj. 2, pp. 18-29, Video)
12.   Ref: (obj. 3, pp. 23-29, Nash interview #3)

Multiple-Choice

Select the single best answer. If more than one answer is required, it will be so indicated.

1. In comparison to other European nations, England
   A. was in the vanguard of the early stages of exploration.
   B. captured Spain's American possessions.
   C. showed little interest in the early stages of exploration.
   D. believed little could be gained in acquiring colonial possessions.

2. A major difference between English and Spanish colonization was
   A. the former was supported privately and the latter had national support.
   B. the former had national support and the latter was privately supported.
   C. the former had support only from the king while the latter had mainly merchant supporters.
   D. England garnered much public support, and Spain did not.

3. A motive for England's exploration by the early seventeenth century was
   A. a desire for ivory and spices.
   B. a desire for new fishing routes.
   C. bounteous land for the taking.
   D. their determination to defeat Spain.

4. Success came to the Virginia Colony with the production of
   A. wheat.
   B. indigo.
   C. tobacco.
   D. sugar.

5. The settlers of the Chesapeake region believed tribes of the region
   A. were an integral part of success in the region.
   B. could easily be captured and used for labor.
   C. stood in the way of the advancement of civilization.
   D. should assimilate into their culture.

6. A major difference between the establishment of the Virginia and Maryland colonies was
   — A. the motive for settlement.
   B. their success as a colony.
   C. the type of schools established.
   D. their cash crops.

7. In a typical colonial Virginia household of the seventeenth century,
   A. continuity could be found among its members.
   B. life seemed stable and secure.
   —C. family relationships were tangled and complex.
   D. religious institutions played an important role in the family's lifestyle.

8. Professor Edmund Morgan stated that a major cause of instability in Jamestown to 1630 was
   A. the low price of tobacco.
   B. the social classes of the settlers.
   — C. the unbalanced sex ratio.
   D. the lack of local political controls.

Essay Questions

9. The Jamestown colonists suffered many difficulties from 1607 to 1624. What changes in the attitudes of colonists and company leaders helped the colony survive? What brought about financial improvements? What political organizations were created? Why did Virginia become a royal colony in 1624?

10. What were the characteristics of the daily life of the Chesapeake to 1660? What were the main problems of maintaining family life? With what results? What characteristics were most unlike England?

11. Choosing one of the English areas of settlement, describe what your lifestyle might have been if you were a woman in the colonial period.

FEEDBACK REPORT

1. C   Ref: (obj. 1, p. 30)
2. A   Ref: (obj. 1, pp. 31-32)
3. C   Ref: (obj. 1, p. 31, Video)
4. C   Ref: (obj. 2, pp. 40-41, Video & "Jamestown Fiasco")
5. C   Ref: (obj. 2, pp. 39, 41-42)
6. A   Ref: (obj. 2, p. 42-43)
7. C   Ref: (obj. 3, pp. 44-45, Video)
8. C   Ref: (obj. 3, Video, Morgan int. #3 & "Jamestown Fiasco")
9.   Ref: (obj.2, pp.38-44, Video, Jamestown, Reader/Lesson 2)
10.   Ref: (obj. 3, pp. 44-45, Video, Morgan int. #2)
11.   Ref: (obj. 3, pp. 44-46, 54, 56, 62, 66, Video)

Multiple-Choice

Select the single best answer. If more than one answer is required, it will be so indicated.

1. The chief difference between the "Puritans" and the "Separatists" was that
    - A. the Puritans sought to cleanse the Anglican Church; the Separatists thought it too corrupt to be saved.
    - B. the Puritans thought the Anglican Church too "popish"; the Separatists thought it not "popish" enough.
    - C. the Puritans favored the higher clergy; the Separatists opposed them.
    - D. the Puritans enjoyed James I's backing; the Separatists did not.

2. When compared to Virginia, the experience in Massachusetts Bay Colony
    - A. provided stability and organization for the Indians.
    - B. showed much planning and preparation.
    - C. floundered because of lack of planning and organization.
    - D. showed how important economic motivation was in establishing a colony.

3. By 1637, the Puritans
    - A. had successfully defeated the tribes of their region.
    - B. were calling for reinforcements from England to fight the Indians.
    - C. were convinced the Indians had been converted.
    - D. saw the Indians accepting their presence.

4. Unlike the Virginians, the colonists of Massachusetts
    - A. were scattered across the colony.
    - B. believed in democratic rule.
    - C. had no status definition in their society.
    - D. incorporated the concept of community welfare into their colony.

5. Participation in New England government was allowed to
    A. the wealthiest of the town only.
    B. Church officials only.
    − C. male Church members.
    D. all citizens.

6. The first attempt in English America to establish an intercolonial political structure was
    A. Stamp Act Congress.
    ⁓ B. Confederation of New England.
    C. Albany Congress.
    D. Dominion of New England.

7. Roger Williams and Anne Hutchinson represented
    A. the success of the "Errand Into the Wilderness."
    ⁓ B. the difficulty in enforcing church policies in the New World.
    C. the concern Puritans had for the Indians.
    D. the homogeneity of thought found among the Puritan colonists.

8. Professor Edmund Morgan claimed that the Puritan way did not last longer because
    A. the new leadership was not as good.
    B. their economic progress was stymied.
    C. England revoked the charter.
    ⁃ D. the rest of the world did not follow their example.

Essay Questions

9. The Puritans left England because their religious, political, and economic positions were threatened. How did they formulate their New World colony to avoid the problems they experienced in England? Why did they demand conformity? What features of their social order were they most successful in accomplishing? What were their greatest problems? Overall, how would you rate the success of the Puritans?

10. How did the Puritans deal with dissent in the cases of Roger Williams and Anne Hutchinson? With what results?

FEEDBACK REPORT

1. A   Ref: (obj. 1, pp. 48-49, Video)
2. B   Ref: (obj. 2, pp. 48-50)
3. A   Ref: (obj. 2, pp. 53-54)
4. D   Ref: (obj. 2, pp. 54-56, Video)
5. C   Ref: (obj. 2, p. 54)
6. B   Ref: (obj. 2, pp. 56-57)
7. B   Ref: (obj. 4, p. 51, Video)
8. D   Ref: (obj. 5, Video, Morgan interview #2)
9.   Ref: (obj. 1 & 3, pp. 48-52, Video, Morgan int. #1)
10.   Ref: (obj. 4, pp. 51-52, Video)

Multiple-Choice

Select the single best answer. If more than one answer is required, it will be so indicated.

1. In establishing a colonial empire in the New World, the Dutch
   A. were motivated by their religious beliefs.
   B. were determined to defeat the Spanish.
   - C. believed New World colonies would enhance their commercial empire.
   D. became the greatest military power in the region.

2. In which colony would an individual have the greatest amount of freedom?
   - A. Pennsylvania
   B. Carolina
   C. New York
   D. Massachusetts

3. Professor Gary Nash pointed out that the Quakers had a strong sense of
   - A. pacifism.
   B. self-righteousness.
   C. sexism.
   D. racism.

4. In the text, Anthony Johnson and his family represent
   A. the positive results of the institution of slavery.
   B. a model of how a black family could achieve success in the New World.
   C. the difficulties facing blacks in America during the seventeenth and eighteenth centuries.
   D. the typical black slave family.

5. The greatest number of arrivals to the New World between the fifteenth and eighteenth centuries came from
    A. Northern and Western Europe.
    B. Southern and Eastern Europe.
    C. Middle East.
    D. Africa.

6. According to Olaudah Equiano's account in the text, the experience of being captured and sold as a slave meant
    A. the opportunity to participate in a more sophisticated society.
    B. the opportunity to start fresh in the New World.
    C. deep psychological and physiological wounds.
    D. the likelihood of death at the hands of the slave ship's crew.

7. For slaves to survive, they
    A. repeatedly attempted to run away.
    B. divorced themselves from their African traditions.
    C. shaped a culture which combined their heritage and present environment.
    D. became robots who depended totally on their masters for survival.

8. In which of the following areas did slaves outnumber whites by the mid-1700s?
    A. Virginia
    B. Maryland
    C. Inter-mountain areas
    D. Coastal low country

9. American slavery is unique
    A. in its definition as a status position.
    B. in its definition as a racial position.
    C. in its inability to define its place in society.
    D. in its humanitarian concerns.

10. The Quakers were most different from other colonists in which of the following ways?
    A. Relations with the English government
    B. Intercolonial relations
    C. Acquisition of land
  – D. Relations with native tribes

Essay Questions

11. If you were immigrating to the New World in the seventeenth century, which colony would you choose? Include a description of your expectations for the New World and the reality of what you faced.

12. Describe the series of events that brought Africans from their native land to a southern colony. Which part of the trade was most difficult? How did English American slavery differ from slavery elsewhere?

FEEDBACK REPORT

1. C   Ref: (obj. 1-2, pp. 58-60)
2. A   Ref: (obj. 3, pp. 63-65)
3. A   Ref: (obj. 3, Video, Nash interview #1)
4. C   Ref: (obj. 5, pp. 70-71)
5. D   Ref: (obj. 5, p. 72, Video)
6. C   Ref: (obj. 5, pp. 73-74)
7. C   Ref: (obj. 5, pp. 77-78, Video)
8. D   Ref: (obj. 5, p. 78)
9. B   Ref: (obj. 5, p. 77, Video)
10. D Ref: (obj. 3, pp. 63-64, Video)
11.   Ref: (obj. 4, see Chapters 2 & 3)
12.   Ref: (obj. 5, pp. 72-82, Video, Nash int. #2)

Multiple-Choice

Select the single best answer. If more than one answer is required, it will be so indicated.

1. Among the factors which contributed to the witchcraft hysteria of Salem were
   A. several direct attacks on the town by Indian tribes.
   B. anxieties produced in the community by socioeconomic changes.
   C. strife between Massachusetts and the surrounding colonies.
   D. the fulfillment of the Puritan mission in the New World.

2. The colonial insurrections associated with the Glorious Revolution revealed
   A. social and political tensions in the colonies.
   B. the maturity of colonial societies.
   C. the attempt of Papists to dominate in the colonies.
   D. the stable stratification of colonial societies.

3. The Dominion of New England
   A. united Papists and Puritans.
   B. found favor with the Puritans.
   C. brought direct English control of the region.
   D. gave greater political power to the colonies.

4. Professor Gary Nash claimed that in the aftermath of Bacon's Rebellion
   A. the Native Americans were in a stronger position.
   B. white society was mended and more unified.
   C. blacks were treated better.
   D. Governor Berkeley regained control for 20 years.

5. During the colonial rivalries between England and France,
   A. native tribes were nonparticipants.
   B. most of the fighting occurred in Canada.
   C. southern English colonies participated in the war.
   D. both sides used Native Americans in the conflict.

6. Professor Edmund Morgan noted that the witchcraft incident in Salem Village was unusual in that
   A. the Puritan leadership so quickly admitted their mistakes.
   B. no men were executed.
   C. the governor ignored the trials.
   D. Puritan ministers supported the accused.

7. The history of the Indian wars of New England and Virginia
   A. brought turbulence and instability for all involved.
   B. left a legacy of harmony between all groups.
   C. left the colonists convinced native tribes would be difficult to conquer.
   D. left the native tribes rejuvenated for the next 100 years.

8. Bacon's Rebellion was caused by
   A. growing dissatisfaction with the British government.
   B. concern that Carolina settlers were taking fertile land.
   C. the growing anger of settlers to Governor Berkeley's policies.
   D. Governor Berkeley's harsh treatment of the Indians.

Essay Question

9. What roles did social, economic, and political factors play in the Salem witchcraft trials? Include your perception of why this event occurred.

FEEDBACK REPORT

1. B   Ref: (obj. 2, pp. 92-93, Video)
2. A   Ref: (obj. 2, pp. 89-91)
3. C   Ref: (obj. 2, p. 89, Video)
4. B   Ref: (obj. 1, Video, Nash interview)
5. D   Ref: (obj. 3, p. 94)
6. A   Ref: (obj. 3, Video, Morgan interview #2)
7. A   Ref: (obj. 1, pp. 82-85, Video, Nash interview)
8. C   Ref: (obj. 1, p. 84, Video)
9.   Ref: (obj. 2, pp. 92-93, Video, Morgan int. #2)

Multiple-Choice

Select the single best answer. If more than one answer is required, it will be so indicated.

1. Among the major reasons for an increase in colonial population during the 1700s was
   A. a high death rate among colonists.
   B. a decrease in native tribes.
   C. an increase in the number of colonies established.
   - D. an increase in the life span of the colonists.

2. Most arrivals to the colonies after 1700
   A. were ministers and merchants.
   B. held strong ties to their native lands.
   - C. were slaves or indentured servants.
   D. were highly educated and economically prosperous.

3. One advantage a middle colony farmer had over his New England counterpart was
   - A. richer soil to plant.
   B. greater protection from native tribes.
   C. having a homogeneous community.
   D. having fewer people farming in his region.

4. Status in the South was determined by
   A. birth.
   B. English ancestry.
   - C. how much land and labor was owned.
   D. political position.

5. Professor Trickel maintained that for New Englanders to prosper they had to
   A. trade within legal channels.
   B. exchange goods in several different places and ways.
   C. supply the middle colonies with fish.
   D. develop iron manufacturing.

6. Artisans in colonial towns
   A. felt frustrated by their training in their crafts.
   B. were guaranteed quick wealth.
   C. were independent of the rest of the town.
   D. sought recognition by the town for their crafts.

7. According to John Locke,
   A. man had the ability to acquire knowledge and improve his position.
   B. God did not trust man to rule himself.
   C. the fate of man had been left to predetermined forces.
   D. society had reached its full maturity.

8. If a colonist read POOR RICHARD'S ALMANACK, he would learn that
   A. religious duty should take precedence over worldly concerns.
   B. hard work could lead to material success.
   C. the afterlife was more important than the present.
   D. success in life was determined by the community one lived in.

9. Followers of the Great Awakening
   A. were those who controlled the reins of power in their individual colonies.
   B. were able to separate other concerns from their religious beliefs.
   C. brought their beliefs into the political and social arena of their colonies.
   D. were confined to a small segment of colonial society.

10. The most important power acquired by colonial legislatures in the eighteenth century was
    A. the right to form a militia.
    B. the right to appoint colonial officials.
    C. the right to initiate legislation.
    D. the right to control the purse strings.

11. According to what British political ideology did too much power in any one person or group cause tyranny and corruption?
    A. Tory ideology
    B. Whig ideology
    C. Democracy
    D. Republicanism

Essay Questions

12. How did the eighteenth-century immigrant to colonial America differ from his seventeenth-century counterpart? Which group of immigrants had a better chance of success? Explain.

13. Analyze the impact of the Great Awakening on colonial life. How did it help to heighten the tensions of the period?

FEEDBACK REPORT

1. D   Ref: (obj. 1, p. 102)
2. C   Ref: (obj. 1, p. 103)
3. A   Ref: (obj. 1, p. 111)
4. C   Ref: (obj. 1, pp. 117-119)
5. B   Ref: (obj. 1, Video, Trickel interview #1)
6. D   Ref: (obj. 2, pp. 122-123, Video)
7. A   Ref: (obj. 3, p. 125)
8. B   Ref: (obj. 3, Video)
9. C   Ref: (obj. 3, pp. 128-131, Video, Trickel interview #2)
10. D   Ref: (obj. 4, p. 139, Video)
11. B   Ref: (obj. 4, p. 140)
12.   Ref: (obj. 1, pp. 102-105)
13.   Ref: (obj. 3, pp. 128-131, 132-133, Video, Trickel int. #2)

Multiple-Choice

Select the single best answer. If more than one answer is required, it will be so indicated.

1. One of the consequences of England's concern with military priorities in the mid-eighteenth century was
    A. a program for internal taxation of England.
    B. more enlistment of colonists into the British army.
    C. the demand for increased revenues from the colonies.
    D. the demand for more immigration to the colonies.

2. Unlike the coastal tribes, the interior tribes of North America
    A. were able to use the European rivalries to their advantage.
    B. were quickly eliminated by the European powers.
    C. moved away from the encroaching European powers.
    D. succumbed to the demands of the Europeans.

3. Pitt's theory for success against the French
    A. called for concentrating British forces in Europe.
    B. ignored the need for tribal alliances.
    C. saw large amounts of troops being sent to America.
    D. meant swift, decisive actions on the high seas.

4. By 1758, the Iroquois realized
    A. it was in their best interests to join in an alliance with the English.
    B. it was in their best interests to join in an alliance with the French.
    C. remaining neutral in the Anglo-French confrontation would protect their tribe.
    D. the colonists would not remain united against the French threat.

5. At the end of the Seven Years' War (French and Indian War) in America, which class suffered the most hardships?
   A. Labor
   B. Upper class
   C. Craftsmen
   D. Farmer

6. Ebenezer MacIntosh represents
   A. one of the well-known figures of the American Revolution.
   B. the wellspring of Americans who supported the American Revolution.
   C. the British who supported the American cause.
   D. those Americans who opposed the American Revolution.

7. For the British government, the Sugar and Stamp Acts
   A. would bring harmony with the colonists.
   B. were necessary to maintain a successful empire.
   C. would place the colonists under the direct control of the monarch.
   D. clarified the role of the colonial assemblies.

8. What effect did the Stamp Act have on the colonies?
   A. It provided an opportunity for new colonial leadership.
   B. It raised large amounts of revenue.
   C. It enhanced the power of colonial elites.
   D. It healed the rift among the social classes of the colonies.

9. Professor Edmund Morgan stated that the colonists opposed British taxation because
   A. it was not their responsibility to pay for defense.
   B. the colonists, without representation, could not control future taxes.
   C. the new taxes were so high.
   D. it stifled their trade.

10. The Declaration of Independence
   A. presented a set of original theories regarding the role of government.
   B. presented a platform for a national government.
   C. presented the prevailing political theories to justify a revolution.
   D. caused great consternation among the colonists.

Essay Questions

11. Explain why many colonists believed a break from England would provide an opportunity to regenerate and reform American society. Include in your answer examples of tensions that were evident in American society by the time of the Revolution.

12. How and why did British imperial policy change toward the colonists after 1763? Might a better policy have been devised to meet their objectives? Explain.

FEEDBACK REPORT

1. C Ref: (obj. 1, p. 147, Video)
2. A Ref: (obj. 1, pp. 148-149, Video)
3. C Ref: (obj. 1, pp. 148-149)
4. A Ref: (obj. 1, p. 149, Video)
5. A Ref: (obj. 1, p. 151, Video)
6. B Ref: (obj. 2, pp. 146, 162, Video)
7. B Ref: (obj. 2, pp. 153-156)
8. A Ref: (obj. 2, pp. 153-159, Video)
9. B Ref: (obj. 2, Video, Morgan interview #1)
10. C Ref: (obj. 2, pp. 167-168)
11.   Ref: (obj. 2 & 3, pp. 161-169, Video)
12.   Ref: (obj. 2, pp. 153-169, Video, Morgan interview #1)

Multiple-Choice

Select the single best answer. If more than one answer is required, it will be so indicated.

1. In the early years of the American Revolution, the Second Continental Congress can be characterized as
   A. a responsible legitimate representative body.
   B. unsure and weak in its role as a representative body.
   C. dominated by Southern representatives who led the war effort.
   D. exercising enormous war powers in order to unite the colonies.

2. Which of the following groups delayed ratification of the Articles of Confederation?
   A. Land speculators
   B. Merchants
   C. Farmers
   D. Soldiers

3. What advantage did the British have in New York?
   A. They were closer to England.
   B. Loyalist sentiment was strong in the region.
   C. Washington would not attack their position.
   D. New York harbor was narrow and difficult to capture.

4. A key reason for the defeat of Cornwallis at Yorktown was
   A. the arrival of the French fleet.
   B. the arrival of Dutch troops.
   C. the lack of strategy by the British.
   D. the alliance of the Americans with the Dutch.

5. The battles of Trenton and Princeton
   A. were decisive victories for General Howe.
   B. gave Washington's army a morale boost.
   C. were indecisive draws.
   D. ended British encroachment into New Jersey.

6. Professor Peter Maslowski maintained that the British military position in the American Revolution was
   A. more tenuous than might be expected.
   B. overwhelmingly superior to the United States.
   C. enhanced by superior leadership.
   D. diminished by an inferior navy.

7. The victory at Saratoga
   A. nearly won the war for England.
   B. cost the United States several thousand lives.
   C. led to an American-French alliance.
   D. led to an American-Iroquois treaty.

8. Among the ingredients of America's Revolutionary War victory were all of the following EXCEPT
   A. militias provided a vast reservoir of manpower.
   B. Washington's amazing administrative and organizational talents.
   C. the support of the majority of native tribes west of the Appalachian Mountains.
   D. the cautious and often inept British leadership.

9. As the war continued, the Continental Army was increasingly
   A. composed of middling farmers from the North.
   B. composed of poor men who joined for personal gain.
   C. composed of foreign immigrants.
   D. motivated by the high ideals of republicanism.

10. What impact did the Revolutionary War have on British Indian allies?
    A. Left them with few, but secure, havens
    B. Totally destroyed all their towns
    C. Actually left them in an improved position due to British continued presence in Canada
    D. Meant clear and devastating defeat

11. Loyalists during the American Revolution were
    A. most numerous in New England.
    B. generally from the artisan class and urban poor.
    C. given recognition and compensation by the treaty ending the Revolution.
    D. most numerous among the upper and middle rank of colonial society.

Essay Questions

12. Explain why the chances of the colonists winning the war seemed slim at the beginning of the American Revolution. Explain what you think the turning point was. Which specific military events led to American success? Why?

13. The United States fought seven (7) years to win its independence. What were the three (3) most significant battles leading to victory? What were the primary impacts of each?

FEEDBACK REPORT

1. B   Ref: (obj. 1, p. 185)
2. A   Ref: (obj. 1, p. 186)
3. B   Ref: (obj. 2, p. 183, Video)
4. A   Ref: (obj. 2, p. 188, Video)
5. B   Ref: (obj. 2, Video, Maslowski interview #2)
6. A   Ref: (obj. 2, Video, Maslowski interview #1)
7. C   Ref: (obj. 2, Video, Maslowski interview #3)
8. C   Ref: (obj. 2, pp. 189-191, Video)
9. B   Ref: (obj. 2, p. 194)
10. D   Ref: (obj. 4, pp. 189-191, Video)
11. D   Ref: (obj. 4, pp. 200-201)
12.   Ref: (obj. 2, TG intro, Video, Maslowski int. #1)
13.   Ref: (obj. 2, Maslowski interviews)

Multiple-Choice

Select the single best answer. If more than one answer is required, it will be so indicated.

1. One of the most important ideas the Revolution was responsible for was
   A. the desire of Americans for total democracy.
   B. the need to define the relationship of liberty and authority.
   C. the need to define the meaning of republicanism.
   D. the need to incorporate disenfranchised groups into the political system.

2. According to the revolutionaries, political order could be maintained
   A. by the ability of the citizenry to be responsible for insuring the welfare of society.
   B. by imposing it through a strong central government.
   C. by a standing army that prevented infractions against society.
   D. by a strong executive branch which would provide national leadership.

3. The most dramatic changes in government during the Revolution occurred on the
   A. local level.
   B. national level.
   C. state level.
   D. county level.

4. The new state constitutions
   A. implemented republicanism as a workable form of government.
   B. were less democratic than their colonial predecessors.
   C. gave increased powers to governors at the expense of the legislatures.
   D. increased the distance between government and the citizens.

5. Among the dilemmas of Revolutionary politics was what to do about all the following EXCEPT
    A. slavery.
    B. separation of church and state.
    C. mounting public debt.
    D. acquisition of new territories.

6. During the Articles of Confederation period, the actions of Spain in the Mississippi River region indicated
    A. the high regard Europeans had for the new nation.
    B. the ineffectiveness of the Congress in foreign relations.
    C. the strength of the American way.
    D. the Americans clearly understood the intricacies of European diplomacy.

7. Professor Forrest McDonald related the demise of the Confederation government to the
    A. Annapolis Convention.
    B. bankruptcy of the confederation.
    C. Rhode Island Paper Money faction.
    D. Potomac Agreement.

8. As economic problems mounted in Massachusetts during the Confederation period,
    A. the legislature acted quickly to find solutions.
    B. frustrated citizens felt they had to take matters into their own hands.
    C. the Congress acted reasonably and fairly.
    D. the courts acted in a fair and responsible manner.

Essay Questions

9. By the mid-1780s, the Federalists believed the nation was in the midst of a social and political crisis that threatened its very survival. Were they correct in their assessment that the revolutionary ideology had failed? What were the immediate problems that seemed so overwhelming? Were the

long-term effects of the period more important than the short-term events? Explain.

10. A significant accomplishment during the period of the Articles of Confederation was a western land policy. Describe the provisions of the two Confederation land acts and explain the importance of each act.

FEEDBACK REPORT

1. B Ref: (obj. 1, p. 205, Video)
2. A Ref: (obj. 1, p. 205)
3. C Ref: (obj. 1, pp. 207-209)
4. A Ref: (obj. 1, pp. 207-209)
5. D Ref: (obj. 2, p. 223, Video)
6. B Ref: (obj. 4, p. 225)
7. B Ref: (obj. 4, Video, McDonald interview #2)
8. B Ref: (obj. 5, pp. 231-233, Video)
9.   Ref: (obj. 1-3, pp. 215-218, 226-233, TG intro, Video)
10.   Ref: (obj. 3, pp. 223-226, Telecourse Guide)

Multiple-Choice

Select the single best answer. If more than one answer is required, it will be so indicated.

1. The delegates to the Constitutional Convention of 1787
   A. had little experience with the reins of government.
   B. were determined to save the Articles of Confederation.
   C. understood the complexities of the task before them.
   D. wanted a public forum to debate the major issues.

2. To the Federalists at the Constitutional Convention,
   A. the political system would be open for all to participate in.
   B. the federal government had to be constructed to insure stability.
   C. the state governments would provide stability.
   D. the political process would be responsible directly to the people.

3. For the Constitution to be accepted,
   A. nine states had to ratify it.
   B. thirteen states had to ratify it.
   C. a majority of the population had to vote for it.
   D. Congress had to approve it.

4. In Federalist Paper No. 10, Madison argues
   A. public good will always be placed first by the people.
   B. compromise could not be achieved by competing interests.
   C. only homogeneity can provide the perfect political state.
   D. public good will be defined by the needs of various competing groups.

5. As the debate for ratification of the constitution raged,
   A. the public seemed confident about the role of the national government.
   B. a sense of uneasiness about the ability of the proposed government to protect the goals of the Revolution emerged.
   C. most felt it would continue the concept of government established by the Confederation.
   D. few seemed aware of the difference between the two forms of government.

6. Professor Forrest McDonald said the Federalists had to overcome what two major objections?
   A. Fear of power and love of liberty
   B. Dissatisfaction with Washington and no Bill of Rights
   C. No Bill of Rights and lack of commercial controls
   D. Too little executive power and too many states' rights

7. Ratification of the Constitution in New York and Virginia indicated
   A. the large pluralities by which it was accepted.
   B. that most Americans participated in the process.
   C. the narrowness of acceptance.
   D. how unprepared the Federalists were.

8. In the Hamiltonian vision of the nation,
   A. an agrarian empire of yeoman farmers would prevail.
   B. the government should not interfere in the economy.
   C. government would foster economic growth and development.
   D. the government should court the support of the lower class.

9. Hamilton's proposal for a bank rested on
   A. strict interpretation of the Constitution.
   B. the implied powers of the Constitution.
   C. the principle of state rights.
   D. the ideology of republicanism.

10. Washington's response to the Whiskey Rebellion
    A. showed his determination to win respect for the new government.
    B. convinced many the new government would not last.
    C. forced Hamilton to resign from office.
    D. failed to quell the rebellion and its supporters.

Essay Questions

11. In order to complete the Constitution of 1787 the delegates agreed to several compromises. What were the major compromises? How did these compromises reflect the sectional/regional divisions of the time? Explain.

12. The ratification of the Constitution was accomplished by careful planning, shrewd bargaining, and good luck. What was this ratification process, and how was it determined? Who were the major writers of THE FEDERALIST PAPERS, and what major points did they make? List and explain three Anti-Federalist objections to the Constitution. Why were the ratifications of Virginia and New York pivotal?

FEEDBACK REPORT

1. C   Ref: (obj. 2, p. 234, Video)
2. B   Ref: (obj. 2, p. 236)
3. A   Ref: (obj. 3, p. 237, Video)
4. D   Ref: (obj. 3, p. 238)
5. B   Ref: (obj. 3, pp. 237-240)
6. A   Ref: (obj. 3, Video, McDonald interview #2)
7. C   Ref: (obj. 3, pp. 239-240)
8. C   Ref: (obj. 5, p. 249, Reader Article for Lesson 10)
9. B   Ref: (obj. 5, pp. 249-252, Reader Article for Lesson 10)
10. A   Ref: (obj. 5, pp. 254-255)
11.   Ref: (obj 2, pp.236-37, Video, McDonald #1, Art. for Ch. 8)
12.   Ref: (obj. 3, pp. 237-243, Video, McDonald intrvw #2)

Multiple-Choice

Select the single best answer. If more than one answer is required, it will be so indicated.

1. By the mid-1790s,
    A. harmony had been maintained through Washington's leadership.
    B. domestic and foreign policies had sharply divided the nation.
    C. little hope remained for the ability of the government to govern.
    D. Britain eagerly waited to regain control of North America.

2. Who was the minister from France who attempted to gain a bribe from American officials in 1797?
    A. Citizen Genet
    B. Premier Tallyrand
    C. General Lafayette
    D. Minister Richelieu

3. In reaction to the XYZ Affair, the Federalists
    A. developed a program against internal and external enemies.
    B. maintained calm in the face of mounting public pressure.
    C. demanded the resignation of Adams.
    D. declared war against France and mounted a successful military campaign.

4. In the text, Luther Baldwin learned in 1798 that
    A. the Sedition Act would have little effect on his life.
    B. civil liberties will not always be protected by the federal government.
    C. patriotism should be legislated by the federal government.
    D. the federal government had little interest in the lives of its citizens.

5. The doctrine of the Virginia and Kentucky Resolutions
   A. amplified the powers of the federal government.
   B. placed final authority in the hands of the states.
   C. gained much support from other regions.
   D. led states to stop enforcing the Alien and Sedition Acts.

6. James Callender was
   A. an advocate of George Washington.
   B. in the secret pay of Alexander Hamilton.
   C. convicted of sedition in biased procedures.
   D. a secret agent for Genet.

7. Professor Forrest McDonald explained that Southern and Western pro-French sentiment was partially a result of
   A. a desire for Florida and Louisiana.
   B. fondness for Genet.
   C. French protection of American rights on the Mississippi.
   D. the French-Spanish alliance.

Essay Questions

8. Why did Americans face a dilemma as war broke out in Europe in the 1790s? Could the nation have avoided the crisis this war created for the new government?

9. What were the Alien and Sedition Acts? Why were they passed? What methods were used to protest their passage and implementation? How was the James Callender case a sign of their use and abuse?

FEEDBACK REPORT

1. B   Ref: (obj. 1, pp. 255-256)
2. B   Ref: (obj. 1, pp. 260-261)
3. A   Ref: (obj. 3, pp. 260-263)
4. B   Ref: (obj. 4, p. 263)
5. B   Ref: (obj. 4, pp. 264-265, Video)
6. C   Ref: (obj. 4, Video, McDonald interview #1)
7. A   Ref: (obj. 4, Video, McDonald interview #1)
8.   Ref: (obj. 1, pp. 255-260, Video)
9.   Ref: (obj. 4, pp. 261-263, Video, McDonald intrvw #1)

Multiple-Choice

Select the single best answer. If more than one answer is required, it will be so indicated.

1. In the first half of the nineteenth century, southern agricultural profits improved dramatically with
   A. the ability to grow and prepare for market short-staple cotton.
   B. a new variety of tobacco.
   C. a flood tide of new indentured servants.
   D. greatly improved fertilizing techniques.

2. Life in early nineteenth century trans-Appalachia was characterized by
   A. widespread poverty and social unrest.
   B. transiency, youthfulness, and predominant maleness.
   C. careful use of resources.
   D. reliance on long-stable cotton for profits.

3. What was the role for women's education in the republic?
   A. Education should be given to a talented few.
   B. Emphasis should be placed on vocational training.
   C. Education should be left to the individual families.
   D. To help women function more effectively within traditional spheres.

4. The Jeffersonian vision of America seemed clouded in the early nineteenth century by
   A. industriousness-generated inequality.
   B. increasing reliance on slavery.
   C. too rapid westward expansion.
   D. larger and larger northeastern farms.

5. Which state leader believed poverty and disease should be attacked through government programs?
   A. DeWitt Clinton
   B. Benjamin Franklin
   C. Robert Fulton
   D. Samuel Adams

6. Most freed blacks in the North
   A. found their lives much improved in the early nineteenth century.
   B. were able to find a place in the artisan communities of the cities.
   C. found life improved, but segregation increasing.
   D. returned to slavery after a short period of time.

7. Professor Julie Jeffrey described all of the following as characteristics of frontier communities, EXCEPT
   A. wastefulness of resources.
   B. faith in the leadership of intellectuals.
   C. tendency toward transience.
   D. faith in equality.

Essay Question

8. You are living in a farming community in eastern Tennessee. Describe the environment in which you live. Did your lifestyle reflect the prevailing ideology of the period?

FEEDBACK REPORT

1. A   Ref: (obj. 1, pp. 286-287)
2. B   Ref: (obj. 1, p. 288)
3. D   Ref: (obj. 2, pp. 298-299)
4. A   Ref: (obj. 2, p. 277)
5. A   Ref: (obj. 1, p. 297)
6. C   Ref: (obj. 3, pp. 303-305)
7. B   Ref: (obj. 3, Video, Jeffrey interview #2)
8.   Ref: (obj. 1, 2, 3, pp. 276-289, Video)

Multiple-Choice

Select the single best answer. If more than one answer is required, it will be so indicated.

1. In order to implement the Republican platform,
   A. Jefferson assumed control of the Judiciary.
   B. Jefferson wanted all three branches to reflect these ideals.
   C. leading Federalist congressmen were impeached.
   D. the powers of the Congress were expanded.

2. The Marshall Court
   A. weakened the authority of the judiciary.
   B. enhanced the powers of the states.
   C. seemed unsure of its role in the federal government.
   D. affirmed the role of the court as a policy maker.

3. The election of 1800 had particular significance, because
   A. a Federalist was administering the oath of office to a Republican.
   B. it was marked by confusion and bloodshed.
   C. power passed peacefully from one political party to another.
   D. few felt loyalty to the new president.

4. Jefferson's foreign policy
   A. tried to steer a course of neutrality during the Napoleonic wars.
   B. singled England out as the primary enemy of the United States.
   C. forged an alliance with the neutral nations of Europe.
   D. de-emphasized the importance of commerce to the American economy.

5. In the early 1800s, tension arose with England concerning
   A. trade agreements.
   B. troops in the western frontier.
   C. impressment of sailors.
   D. closing of British ports.

6. The effects of the Embargo Act were felt most by
   A. England.
   B. France.
   C. Latin America.
   D. the United States.

7. The War of 1812
   A. is one of the most well-defined wars the U.S. has fought.
   B. proved the effectiveness of American foreign policy.
   C. provided the nation with an opportunity to demonstrate its military superiority.
   D. found its results more important than the war itself.

8. The Treaty of Ghent (1814)
   A. resolved the differences between England and the U.S.
   B. ended the fighting. *endwar of 1812*
   C. proved the might and power of the U.S. to the European nations.
   D. guaranteed U.S. recognition as a major world power.

9. What did the United States receive as a result of the War of 1812, according to Professor Peter Maslowski?
   A. Nothing
   B. New Orleans
   C. A shattering of the Indian confederation
   D. A clear-cut victory over Spain

Essay Questions

10. As Jefferson took office, he proclaimed, "We are all Federalists, we are all Republicans." Did his actions as a president support this statement? Include examples of how he shaped the government once in office.

11. Explain why the United States went to war with England in 1812. What did the United States achieve militarily in the war? Diplomatically? Why was the end of the war a significant turning point for the Republic?

FEEDBACK REPORT

1. B   Ref: (obj. 1, pp. 273-274)
2. D   Ref: (obj. 1, pp. 274-275)
3. C   Ref: (obj. 1, p. 273)
4. A   Ref: (obj. 2, p. 306, Video)
5. C   Ref: (obj. 2, p. 306, Video)
6. D   Ref: (obj. 2, p. 306, Video)
7. D   Ref: (obj. 2, pp. 308-309, Video)
8. B   Ref: (obj. 2, p. 308, Video)
9. C   Ref: (obj. 2, Video, Maslowski interview #2)
10.   Ref: (obj. 1, pp. 273-277, Video)
11.   Ref: (obj. 2, pp. 305-309, Video, Maslowski intrvws #1, #2)

Multiple-Choice

Select the single best answer. If more than one answer is required, it will be so indicated.

1. The Monroe Doctrine
   A. dramatically affected the U.S. position in the Western Hemisphere.
   B. caused European powers to respect U.S. policy.
   C. aligned the U.S. and England in Latin American policies.
   D. laid the foundation for later dominance of the U.S. in the Western Hemisphere.

2. Professor K. Jack Bauer explained that the vigorous foreign policy following the War of 1812 was a result of
   A. American confidence that its system was the wave of the future.
   B. America's belief that it was militarily superior.
   C. the expanded naval fleet that gave security.
   D. Jackson's victory at New Orleans.

3. In the Monroe Doctrine, the president asserted ALL the following, EXCEPT
   A. the American continents were closed to new colonization.
   B. the United States would oppose any extension of European influence in the Americas.
   C. the United States would support British policy in the Americas.
   D. the United States would not interfere with existing colonies in America.

4. Post-war of 1812 politics were characterized by
   A. a surge of voter participation.
   B. relaxation of property qualifications, but retained tax requirements.
   C. increased participation of women and educated African-Americans.
   D. a resurgence in Federalist voters.

5. The Missouri Compromise
    A. temporarily quelled the fires fanned by the slavery issue.
    B. gave the nation a long term solution for the slavery issue.
    C. brought the nation to the brink of the Civil War.
    D. pointed out how rapidly the South had gained control of the Congress.

6. The Panic of 1819 was a result of ALL the following EXCEPT
    A. overspeculation by western farmers.
    B. drought in Europe.
    C. credit policies of the Bank of the United States.
    D. overproduction of cotton.

7. The main goal of federal Indian policy in the early 1800s was
    A. to Christianize the tribes.
    B. to secure the natives from the advancing white population.
    C. to reduce conflict among the tribes.
    D. the acquisition of Native American land.

8. The late eighteenth and early nineteenth centuries fur trade
    A. did little good for white society.
    B. had severe results for the natives.
    C. produced significant wealth for the natives.
    D. had virtually no impact on trans-Appalachia natives.

9. The Iroquois prophet, Handsome Lake, advocated
    A. resistance.
    B. accommodation.
    C. assimilation.
    D. separation.

10. Native resistance in the old Southwest was virtually ended at
    A. Tippecanoe Creek.
    B. the Battle of New Orleans.
    C. Horseshoe Bend.
    D. Fallen Timbers.

Essay Question

11. The United States experienced an upsurge in nationalism following the War of 1812. Cite specific examples of nationalistic tendencies in foreign affairs and domestic affairs in this period. Explain.

FEEDBACK REPORT

1. D   Ref: (obj. 2, p. 309)
2. A   Ref: (obj. 2, Video, Bauer interview #1)
3. C   Ref: (obj. 2, p. 309)
4. A   Ref: (obj. 2, pp. 309-310)
5. A   Ref: (obj. 3, pp. 312-313)
6. B   Ref: (obj. 3, Telecourse Guide, Video)
7. D   Ref: (obj. 3, pp. 289-290)
8. B   Ref: (obj. 3, p. 290)
9. B   Ref: (obj. 3, p. 292)
10. C   Ref: (obj. 3, pp. 294-295)
11.   Ref: (obj. 2, pp. 306-309, Telecourse Guide intro., Video)

Multiple-Choice

Select the single best answer. If more than one answer is required, it will be so indicated.

1. What accounted for the increase in productivity and national wealth between 1820-1860?
    A. The United States was able to import abundant amounts of natural resources.
    B. New sources of labor were found in Native American tribes.
    C. The size of American families dramatically increased, providing new labor supplies.
    D. Increases in population and natural resources provided an economic base.

2. What was one method the federal government used to foster economic growth?
    A. It protected the economy from foreign investors.
    B. It built a national railroad system.
    C. It lowered the tariff.
    D. It provided economic stimulation through its tariff policies.

3. Most Americans felt industrialization had
    A. brought more problems than they had anticipated.
    B. made America a more complex society than in the eighteenth century.
    C. brought benefits to a small percentage of society.
    D. placed America on the road to a utopian society.

4. The majority of the work force in the Lowell mills were
    A. children.
    B. men.
    C. women.
    D. immigrants.

5. As women entered the work force,
   A. bonding occurred as they shared the experience.
   B. competition was fierce as they reached for new opportunities.
   C. men felt threatened by their presence in the work force.
   D. a hierarchal order between older and younger women workers was established.

6. Professor Julie Jeffrey said the most crucial change in American work the first half of the 1800s was the
   A. beginning of women working in factories.
   B. way goods were produced.
   C. increased use of skilled labor.
   D. decrease in educational opportunities.

7. How can farming be characterized between 1820 and 1860?
   A. Farmers' productivity declined.
   B. Farmers felt alienated by the economic changes of the period.
   C. Family farms rapidly decreased as commercialization took place.
   D. Rural life patterns were transformed by the economic needs of the period.

8. By 1820, federal Indian policy
   A. favored the needs of Native Americans.
   B. exploited Native Americans.
   C. clearly defined the tribe's place in society.
   D. seemed confusing and ambivalent regarding Native Americans.

9. What policy did the Cherokees devise for survival?
   A. Assimilation
   B. Disappearance
   C. Accommodation
   D. Segregation

10. The "Trail of Tears" was part of the removal of the
    A. Cherokee Indians.
    B. Creek Indians.
    C. Chickasaw Indians.
    D. Seminole Indians.

Essay Questions

11. In what ways did industrialization bring more than economic changes to American society? You may want to include in your answer changes that occurred in norms, values, family, and societal order.

12. What strategies did Native Americans develop to respond to the changes of the 1800s? Were any of them successful?

FEEDBACK REPORT

1. D   Ref: (obj. 1, pp. 322-326)
2. D   Ref: (obj. 1, p. 322)
3. B   Ref: (obj. 1, pp. 327-328)
4. C   Ref: (obj. 1, p. 331, Video)
5. A   Ref: (obj. 1, pp. 332-335, Video)
6. B   Ref: (obj. 1, Video, Jeffrey interview #1)
7. D   Ref: (obj. 4, pp. 351-353)
8. D   Ref: (obj. 5, pp. 289-292, Video)
9. C   Ref: (obj. 5, p. 292)
10. A   Ref: (obj. 5, pp. 404-405, Video)
11.   Ref: (obj. 1, Video, Jeffrey interview #1)
12.   Ref: (obj. 5, Text pp. 289-295, Video, Edmunds intrvw #1)

Multiple-Choice

Select the single best answer. If more than one answer is required, it will be so indicated.

1. The experience of Frederick Douglass's life as a slave
   A. indicates how difficult the institution was for both master and slave.
   B. depicts the kindness of the master towards the slave.
   C. points out how whites perceived slavery as a system of labor.
   D. indicates the gulf which existed between slave and master.

2. How did the typical white southerner live during the antebellum period?
   A. In an opulent mansion with hundreds of slaves in the fields
   B. On a small farm with no slaves to help in the fields
   C. In the cities and was involved in commercial activity
   D. On a dairy farm producing food supplies for the city

3. What effect did the invention of the cotton gin have on the South?
   A. It allowed the region to diversify.
   B. It made slavery an institution that would help the South maximize its profits.
   C. It forced vast numbers of poor whites off their farms.
   D. It tied the South to an agricultural commodity which would bring small economic rewards.

4. What did the increasing value of the slave during the antebellum period indicate?
   A. The decreasing number of slaves available to planters
   B. The high failure rate among the planter class
   C. The attempt to diversify the economy of the South
   D. The faith of the planter in the agricultural system of the South

5. Perhaps the worst feature of slavery was the
   A. political inequality.
   B. physical harm.
   C. psychological effect.
   D. economic inequality.

6. The relationship between slave owner and slave
   A. was defined by the legal codes of the South.
   B. followed Judaic-Christian traditions.
   C. was based on the economic value of slaves.
   D. varied from household to household.

7. Professor Alphine Jefferson said that slavery was harsh and inflexible in order to
   A. keep the blacks working.
   B. break the slave's spirit.
   C. discourage marriage.
   D. stop runaways.

8. Why was the family important to the slave community?
   A. It taught them how to be assimilated into white society.
   B. Slave families were given preferential treatment by slave owners.
   C. It provided unity and stability for its members.
   D. It protected its members from the master.

9. According to Professor Alphine Jefferson, what was the double meaning of the Brer Rabbit tales?
   A. They helped keep the masters happy.
   B. They entertained the white folks.
   C. They taught black children how to read.
   D. They helped socialize and educate slave children.

10. Free blacks in the South
    A. found freedom a liberating experience.
    B. became economically prosperous.
    C. decreased in number during the antebellum period.
    D. found freedom difficult and lonely.

Essay Questions

11. Frederick Douglass observed, "You cannot outlaw one part of the people without endangering the rights and liberties of all people." Explain how slavery became more than a labor system in the South, including how it limited the opportunities of whites.

12. In spite of the hardships faced, slaves were able to maintain a level of self-esteem and stability. To what do you attribute their success? How important were family, folk tales, and religion to the slave? Explain.

FEEDBACK REPORT

1. A   Ref: (obj. 1, pp. 358-359, 364)
2. B   Ref: (obj. 1, p. 360)
3. B   Ref: (obj. 1, p. 361)
4. D   Ref: (obj. 1, p. 363)
5. C   Ref: (obj. 2, pp. 373)
6. D   Ref: (obj. 2, pp. 376-378, Video)
7. A   Ref: (obj. 2, Video, Jefferson interview #1)
8. C   Ref: (obj. 3, pp. 382-383, Video)
9. D   Ref: (obj. 3, Video, Jefferson interview #2)
10. D   Ref: (obj. 5, pp. 388-391)
11.   Ref: (obj. 2, Textbook pp. 363-367, Video)
12.   Ref: (obj 3,4, pp.382-386,Video, Jefferson #2)

Multiple-Choice

Select the single best answer. If more than one answer is required, it will be so indicated.

1. How can the political system of the antebellum period be described?
   A. It was composed of a coalition of elite groups who dominated the system.
   B. It seemed outdated in light of the other changes occurring in society.
   C. It made significant changes in its election procedures.
   D. It left the responsibility of government in the hands of a talented few.

2. How had Andrew Jackson acquired a national reputation before becoming president?
   A. Through his economic achievements
   B. By promoting the cause of Native Americans
   C. By his achievements in the U.S. Senate
   D. By his military exploits

3. Which section of the country opposed protective tariffs?
   A. South
   B. New England
   C. Middle Atlantic states
   D. Trans-Appalachian West

4. According to Calhoun's "Exposition and Protest",
   A. the ultimate authority of the nation was the federal government.
   B. the ultimate authority of the nation was the states.
   C. the public should participate in governmental decisions.
   D. the courts should intercede if the federal government exceeds its power.

5. In Jackson's opinion, the Bank of the United States
   A. should be rechartered.
   B. had little understanding of the common people's needs.
   C. could be manipulated by him.
   D. should develop policies to foster foreign trade.

6. As a Whig, by 1832 you were convinced
   A. that the nation had to be saved from Andrew Jackson.
   B. that, for the good of the nation, Andrew Jackson had to be re-elected.
   C. that the Bank of the United States should not be rechartered.
   D. that local issues were far more important than national ones.

7. Professor Edward Pessen found the most significant supporters of Andrew Jackson were
   A. frontier aristocrats.
   B. working men in the cities.
   C. southern planters.
   D. northern merchants.

Essay Questions

8. Was Andrew Jackson a demagogue or a hero as president? Looking at the major issues of his administration, did he act in the best interest of the common man? Explain.

9. America has gradually become more "democratic" over the years. Compare and contrast the progress of democracy during the Jeffersonian and Jacksonian periods. What were the most beneficial results of each? What peoples were still left out of the political structure? Why?

10. Nullification was not a new theory in 1828, but was most clearly expressed by John C. Calhoun following the passage of the Tariff of 1828. What was Calhoun's theory and how was it designed to protect a minority interest? What happened when it was attempted in 1832? What was the outcome of the controversy?

FEEDBACK REPORT

1. C   Ref: (obj. 1, pp. 399-400, Video)
2. D   Ref: (obj. 1, p. 400, Video)
3. A   Ref: (obj. 1, pp. 402-404, Video)
4. B   Ref: (obj. 2, p. 403, Video)
5. B   Ref: (obj. 3, p. 405)
6. A   Ref: (obj. 3, p. 406)
7. A   Ref: (obj. 1, Video, Pessen interview #1)
8.   Ref: (obj. 1,2,3, Text pp. 400-408, Video, Pessen int. #1)
9.   Ref: (obj. 4, Jackson, pp. 398-402, Pessen interview)
10.   Ref: (obj. 2, Text pp. 402-404, Pessen int., chapter intro)

Multiple-Choice

Select the single best answer. If more than one answer is required, it will be so indicated.

1. As a follower of Charles Finney, one
    A. should be committed to internal salvation.
    B. must do God"s work by concrete deeds.
    C. would move among Native Americans converting them to Christianity.
    D. would believe in predestination and original sin.

2. As a believer in the teachings of Joseph Smith, which of the following would be correct?
    A. The Bible was the only source of finding God"s word.
    B. Salvation would be achieved only at death.
    C. All children of the world were Satan"s children.
    D. God"s new kingdom had been ordained for America.

3. To the working class, the institution(s) most in need of reform was/were
    A. education.
    B. prisons.
    C. hospitals.
    D. factories.

4. What difficulties did the abolitionist and women"s movements face?
    A. Their goals were difficult to achieve.
    B. They were unable to define their goals.
    C. They had little support form religious groups.
    D. Both used violent methods to achieve their goals.

5. Most white northerners in the 1830s and 1840s
    A. supported the abolitionist movement.
    B. treated blacks as equals.
    C. held the same racial prejudices as southerners.
    D. belonged to the underground railroad system.

---

6. The Seneca Falls meeting of 1848
    A. demanded that slavery be abolished.
    B. demanded that the concept of "domesticity" be legalized.
    C. demanded that women be allowed to join the abolitionist movement.
    D. defined what a woman''s role in society should be.

7. Professor Harvey Graff related ALL of the following to the burst of Jacksonian reform EXCEPT
    A. the Enlightenment stress on human perfectability.
    B. Republican individualism and egalitarianism.
    C. the traditional Calvinism of Finney.
    D. the young trying to find a "sense of themselves."

8. This American believed in the immediate abolition of slavery.
    A. Henry Clay
    B. William Lloyd Garrison
    C. George Fitzhugh
    D. Charles Finney

Essay Questions

9. What were the major impulses for the antebellum reform movements? Specifically describe three forces influencing reform and three movements influenced by these forces.

10. Why did Jacksonian politics and antebellum reform occur at the same time? Explain.

FEEDBACK REPORT

1. B   Ref: (obj. 1, p. 396-397, Video)
2. D   Ref: (obj. 1, pp. 414-415)
3. D   Ref: (obj. 4, p. 419)
4. A   Ref: (obj. 4, pp. 420-428, Video)
5. C   Ref: (obj. 4, p. 424)
6. D   Ref: (obj. 4, pp. 420-428, Video)
7. C   Ref: (obj. 4, Video, Graff interview #1)
8. B   Ref: (obj. 4, p. 421, Video)
9.   Ref: (obj. 4, pp. 412-416, Video, Graff int #1)
10.   Ref: (obj. 4, p. 430 (conclusion), Video, Graff intrvw #1)

Multiple-Choice

Select the single best answer. If more than one answer is required, it will be so indicated.

1. A major difference between immigrants to agricultural and mining communities was
   A. the former attracted a younger age group.
   B. the latter attracted unmarried individuals.
   C. the former had difficulty establishing stability in their communities.
   D. the latter was more likely to have a very wealthy population.

2. Professor K. Jack Bauer interpreted American attitudes about western movement as
   A. callously indifferent.
   B. an extension of their national mission.
   C. blatant lust for land.
   D. liberation of subject Indians.

3. What was the policy of the federal government toward the Plains tribes?
   A. The government attempted to eliminate all Plains tribes.
   B. The government offered them "protective custody."
   C. The government turned the responsibility to the United States cavalry.
   D. The government offered to replenish buffalo herds.

4. "White Americans" attitude toward Native Americans can best be described as
   A. desirous of assimilating them into society.
   B. concerned for their welfare as expansionism occurred.
   C. believing that the natives were inferior.
   D. concerned that the federal government develop a clear policy regarding their plight.

5. To Lewis Cass, and many other Americans, expansionism meant
   A. individual and national opportunity.
   B. the nation would be faced with many problems.
   C. the western states would dominate the Congress.
   D. opportunity for all groups on the American continent.

6. Why were American settlers attracted to Texas in the 1820s?
   A. They believed there was potential trade with the Indians.
   B. Cotton could be grown on its cheap and available land.
   C. It had natural seaports for commercial trade.
   D. The Mexican government would be more democratic than the American government.

7. In Texas, by the beginning of the 1830s,
   A. American settlers had acquired Mexican citizenship.
   B. American settlers began to express their discontent over Mexican rule.
   C. American slaves had rebelled against the Mexican government.
   D. Americans had found limitless economic opportunities in Texas.

8. A major consideration which forced the delay of the annexation of Texas was
   A. Mexico"s threat of war if Texas was annexed.
   B. the unwillingness of the Texans to be annexed.
   C. Jackson"s strong opposition to annexation.
   D. the fact that Texas would enter the Union as a slave state.

9. The election of 1844
   A. showed how divided the Democratic party was.
   B. gave the Whig party control of the national government.
   C. indicated the public"s sentiments toward Manifest Destiny.
   D. split the nation into opposing sectional camps.

10. The acquisition of the Oregon Territory was resolved
    A. by war between the joint occupiers.
    B. through a negotiated settlement.
    C. through a resolution of Parliament.
    D. because of Polk"s angry denunciation of the British.

Essay Questions

11. Contrast the farming and mining settlements of the West during the antebellum period. Which was most able to duplicate the socio-political communities of the East? Explain.

12. Was the Mexican War a necessary complement to westward expansion? Explain.

FEEDBACK REPORT

1. B   Ref: (obj. 4, p. 454)
2. B   Ref: (obj. 4, Video, Bauer interview #1)
3. C   Ref: (obj. 4, p. 464)
4. C   Ref: (obj. 4, p. 461)
5. A   Ref: (obj. 1, pp. 432-33)
6. B   Ref: (obj. 1, p. 437)
7. B   Ref: (obj. 1, pp. 436-437)
8. D   Ref: (obj. 1, pp. 439-440 & "Texas Must Be Ours")
9. C   Ref: (obj. 1, p. 440, Video)
10. B   Ref: (obj. 2, pp. 443-445, Video)
11.   Ref: (obj. 4, Textbook pp. 452-456)
12.   Ref: (obj. 3, Text pp. 440-443, Video, Bauer interview #2)

Multiple-Choice

Select the single best answer. If more than one answer is required, it will be so indicated.

1. Prior to the 1850s, how had the nation resolved national issues relating to slavery?
    A. Americans were more concerned with the conquest of Native Americans and Mexicans.
    B. Political compromise had resolved these issues.
    C. Economic opportunity had diverted the attention of most Americans.
    D. Frustrations were channeled into the conquest of western territories.

2. The Wilmot Proviso
    A. formed harmony between the sections over the issue of slavery in new territories.
    B. saw the congressmen divide along party lines.
    C. indicated how strong the rift between the sections had become.
    D. ended the Mexican War and allowed Mexicans to become citizens.

3. According to the political arguments of John C. Calhoun, slavery
    A. should be protected by the Congress.
    B. should be abolished by the Congress.
    C. would die a natural death.
    D. should not be allowed into new territories.

4. American politics by 1850 was
    A. rooted in the tradition of republican ideals.
    B. seeing the introduction of new political theories.
    C. broadening its base to incorporate new groups.
    D. redefining the role of the national government.

5. The Compromise of 1850
   A. provided a lasting solution keeping slavery out of national politics.
   B. gave John C. Calhoun what he wanted.
   C. maintained the balance of free and slave states in the Congress.
   D. provided the nation with a respite from the sectional crisis.

6. The most controversial section of the Compromise of 1850 was
   A. the Fugitive Slave Act.
   B. the abolition of slave trade in Washington, D.C.
   C. the admittance of California as a free state.
   D. to have New Mexico organize by popular sovereignty.

7. Professor Eric Foner stated that one of the results of the Compromise of 1850 was
   A. the end of sectional feelings over slavery in the Mexican cession.
   B. to enhance the reputation of Zachary Taylor.
   C. the rise of Stephen Douglas as the major compromise politician.
   D. an end to the question of fugitive slaves.

8. The publication of *Uncle Tom's Cabin* pointed out that
   A. few people were concerned with the issues of the day.
   B. the politicians had understood the attitude of the American people.
   C. the Compromise of 1850 had been successful.
   D. the passions of the 1850s could lead to a national crisis.

Essay Questions

9. While the theory of Manifest Destiny and the expansionism that accompanied it tended to unite the country through the sheer acquisition of new territory, expansionism also acted as a divisive force because it revived the issue of slavery. Discuss the Compromise of 1850 in light of both expansionism and sectional strife over the slavery question. What were the strongest forces in the acceptance of the compromise? Discuss each provision of the compromise.

FEEDBACK REPORT

1. B   Ref: (obj. 2, p. 472, Video, Foner interview)
2. C   Ref: (obj. 2, pp. 472-474, Video)
3. A   Ref: (obj. 2, pp. 473-474, Video)
4. B   Ref: (obj. 3, pp. 473-474)
5. D   Ref: (obj. 3, pp. 475, 478-479, Video)
6. A   Ref: (obj. 3, p. 478-479)
7. C   Ref: (obj. 3, Video, Foner interview #2)
8. D   Ref: (obj. 3, pp. 480-481)
9.   Ref: (obj. 1, 2, and 3, textbook pp. 475, 478-479)

Multiple-Choice

Select the single best answer. If more than one answer is required, it will be so indicated.

1. Which of the following was NOT a factor in weakening the national party system during the 1850s?
   A. The parties denounced the Compromise of 1850.
   B. It was becoming difficult to find patronage jobs during the decade.
   C. Railroad building increased during the period.
   D. Economic prosperity abounded during the period.

2. In winning passage of the Kansas-Nebraska Act, Douglas
   A. brought national recognition to the concept of popular sovereignty.
   B. had understood the temper of the times.
   C. avoided the problems of the Compromise of 1850.
   D. laid to rest the slavery controversy.

3. The settlement of Kansas
   A. cooled sectional tempers.
   B. heightened sectional tempers.
   C. was directed by Congress.
   D. provoked a constitutional crisis.

4. Charles Sumner's speech of "The Crime Against Kansas"
   A. assuaged the southern feelings toward the North.
   B. became the standard bearer for pro-southern settlers in Kansas.
   C. brought the Congress into the troubles of the Kansas issue.
   D. forced the President to take a stand on the Kansas crisis.

5. Professor Kathryn Sklar explained that the slavery issue among Kansas settlers was
   A. insignificant to most.
   B. only an issue to southerners.
   C. a real issue to most settlers.
   D. solved due to John Brown's activities.

6. The newly formed Republican party can best be described as
   A. a reactionary movement to thwart the changes of the period.
   B. rooted in the ideals of Jeffersonian agrarianism.
   C. a coalition of northerners and westerners who had no other political home.
   D. unable to build popular support for its beliefs.

7. The attention of the filibusters was toward
   A. China.
   B. Europe.
   C. Latin America.
   D. Canada.

8. Why did Catholic immigrants gravitate to the Democratic party?
   A. The party took a laissez-faire position regarding social issues.
   B. The party was opposed to slavery.
   C. The party sponsored labor legislation.
   D. The party sponsored naturalization legislation.

Essay Questions

9. Stephen A. Douglas did not expect his Kansas-Nebraska Act to be controversial. What were his reasons for introducing the bill? Why did the act renew sectional controversy? What was the impact of the passage of the act on Kansas, political parties, and Congress?

FEEDBACK REPORT

1. A   Ref: (obj. 1, pp. 481-482)
2. A   Ref: (obj. 2, pp. 482-483)
3. B   Ref: (obj. 2, pp. 488-489, Video)
4. C   Ref: (obj. 2, p. 490, Video)
5. C   Ref: (obj. 2, Video, Sklar interview #1)
6. C   Ref: (obj. 2, p. 487, Video)
7. C   Ref: (obj. 1, pp. 484-485)
8. A   Ref: (obj. 1, p. 486, Video)
9.   Ref: (obj. 2, text pp. 482-483, Video, Sklar interview #1)

Multiple-Choice

Select the single best answer. If more than one answer is required, it will be so indicated.

1. An analysis of the Lincoln-Douglas debates of 1858 indicated
   A. Lincoln was for the immediate abolition of slavery.
   B. Lincoln was no match for Douglas's debating skill.
   C. Douglas's concern for the fate of the slaves.
   D. Douglas's strong support for the concept of popular sovereignty.

2. Professor Kathryn Sklar believes the Lincoln-Douglas debates
   A. helped Lincoln establish a viable moral position on slavery.
   B. gave Douglas an opportunity to re-establish popular sovereignty.
   C. did little to change prevailing opinions.
   D. established the clear superiority of the Dred Scott decision.

3. As a result of the Dred Scott decision,
   A. the Supreme Court was able to resolve the slavery issue.
   B. only the concept of popular sovereignty could apply in the territories.
   C. the Supreme Court supported the principles of the Missouri Compromise.
   D. slavery could not be banned in the territories.

4. The result of John Brown's raid on Harpers Ferry was
   A. slave revolts in the South.
   B. anger in the North at his actions.
   C. fear in the South.
   D. support for the southern Unionist cause.

5. The Republican platform of 1860
   A. promised the abolition of slavery.
   B. emphasized the economic potential of the nation.
   C. promised equal rights for all Americans.
   D. drew moderate southern support.

6. How were the Republicans mistaken in 1860?
   A. They overestimated the Unionist sentiment in the South.
   B. They chose the wrong candidates.
   C. They were unable to win far western support.
   D. They believed sectionalism would prevail.

7. At his inaugural address, Abraham Lincoln
   A. called for the abolition of slavery throughout the nation.
   B. warned that nationalism would triumph over sectionalism.
   C. offered a compromise to the southern states.
   D. impressed Frederick Douglass as a strong, dominant executive.

Essay Questions

8. Could a peaceful resolution have been found for the crisis of the nation by 1860? Explain.

9. Would it be correct to state no single factor caused the Civil War? Support your answer with evidence of what factor(s) converged to break down national unity by 1860.

FEEDBACK REPORT

1. D Ref: (obj. 2, pp. 494-496, Video)
2. A Ref: (obj. 2, Video, Sklar interview #1)
3. D Ref: (obj. 1, pp. 493-494)
4. C Ref: (obj. 3, pp. 496-497, Video)
5. B Ref: (obj. 4, p. 498, Video)
6. A Ref: (obj. 4, p. 499)
7. B Ref: (obj. 5, p. 501)
8.   Ref: (obj. 5, textbook pp. 493-503, Video, Sklar int. #2)
9.   Ref: (obj. 1-5, text pp. 493-503, Video, Sklar intrvw #2)

Multiple-Choice

Select the single best answer. If more than one answer is required, it will be so indicated.

1. President Lincoln's response to the firing on Fort Sumter resulted in
   A. massive numbers of slaves fleeing the South.
   B. an outpouring of support by the Upper South for war.
   C. an outpouring of support by northern whites to take action against the South.
   D. the New England states declaring the war wanton and unjust.

2. The South's greatest asset as the war began was
   A. its industries.
   B. the availability of capital.
   C. a constantly growing population.
   D. its military leaders.

3. As they took office, both Jefferson Davis and Abraham Lincoln
   A. had well-organized governments.
   B. faced organizational problems.
   C. had well-established cabinets.
   D. put their friends into office.

4. The first important Union victories came in
   A. the eastern campaign.
   B. the western campaign.
   C. the Gulf Coast campaign.
   D. the Upper South campaign.

5. Professor Peter Maslowski explained the duration of the Civil War was due, in part, to the
   A. Confederacy's superior numbers.
   B. North's overwhelming advantages.
   C. extraordinary difficulty confronting the Union.
   D. Union's superior generalship.

6. In issuing the Emancipation Proclamation, Lincoln hoped
   A. to shorten the war.
   B. to quiet the abolitionists.
   C. to keep the border states.
   D. to win southern support.

7. The Battle of Gettysburg
   A. marked a turning point in the tide of the war.
   B. meant England and France would become allies of the South.
   C. resulted in the capture of Philadelphia by Lee.
   D. forced Lee's army to surrender.

8. Secretary of State William Seward's main foreign policy objective was
   A. to gain diplomatic recognition from England and France.
   B. to prevent diplomatic recognition of the Confederacy.
   C. to have England and France as military allies.
   D. to force England and France to take sides in the war.

9. Grant's military strategy
   A. followed traditional military tactics.
   B. called for a major decisive battle.
   C. called for continuing the war for several more years.
   D. called for using northern resources to wear down the enemy.

10. When manpower became critical in the war effort,
    A. both governments resorted to the draft.
    B. the South relied on new immigrants.
    C. enlistment rates dramatically increased.
    D. large numbers of slaves joined both armies.

Essay Questions

11. Compare the resources of the North and South as the war began. To what do you attribute the ability of the South to sustain the war effort for four years? What were the primary reasons for the Union's eventual military victory? Explain.

FEEDBACK REPORT

1. C   Ref: (obj. 1, p. 506, Video)
2. D   Ref: (obj. 1, p. 507, Video)
3. B   Ref: (obj. 1, pp. 510-511)
4. B   Ref: (obj. 2, pp. 514-515, Video)
5. C   Ref: (obj. 2, Video, Maslowski interview #1)
6. A   Ref: (obj. 3, p. 521, Video, Maslowski interview #2)
7. A   Ref: (obj. 2, p. 524, Video)
8. B   Ref: (obj. 3, p. 517)
9. D   Ref: (obj. 3, p. 525)
10. A   Ref: (obj. 3, p. 518)
11.   Ref: (obj.2, Ch. 16, pp. 507-508, 525, Video, Maslowski #1)

Multiple-Choice

Select the single best answer. If more than one answer is required, it will be so indicated.

1. One of the unexpected changes the war brought to the North was
   A. a national currency.
   B. greater powers to the Congress.
   C. a rapid deterioration of major industries.
   D. an agricultural depression.

2. Conscription and taxes in the South
   A. helped the war effort.
   B. hindered the war effort.
   C. had little effect on the war effort.
   D. brought immediate relief to the army.

3. Professor Harvey Graff pointed out that the economic impact of the Civil War on the North was
   A. immediate prosperity.
   B. to weld the upper and lower classes together.
   C. felt differently by upper and lower classes.
   D. to cause a prolonged recession.

4. In the 1864 election,
   A. the Democrats portrayed themselves as the party of victory.
   B. the Republicans sought to regain power.
   C. Lincoln believed he could easily win reelection.
   D. military victories helped determine the outcome.

5. For women, the Civil War meant
   A. greater economic freedom.
   B. little change in their lives.
   C. the opportunity to gain political equality.
   D. no longer could they live by the code of domesticity.

---

6. One of the greatest enemies the Confederate government faced was
   A. Grant.
   B. freed slaves.
   C. the slave owners.
   D. Confederate governors.

7. In 1865 most Americans believed that _____ had triumphed with the end of the war.
   A. sectionalism
   B. nationalism
   C. militarism
   D. confederalism

8. According to Professor Eric Foner, the Civil War's impact on northern politics included
   A. establishing its parameters for decades to come.
   B. a weakening of the Republican Party.
   C. elimination of the Democratic Party machines.
   D. a renewed spirit of social reform.

Essay Questions

9. Describe the changes the Civil War brought to northern and southern societies. Analyze the impact these changes made on the lives of the people.

10. Compare and contrast the economic impact of the Civil War on the North and the South. Which was most seriously affected? What elements of the Union had the most benefits? The least?

FEEDBACK REPORT

1. A   Ref: (obj. 1, p. 529)
2. B   Ref: (obj. 1, p. 533)
3. C   Ref: (obj. 1, Video, Graff interview #1)
4. D   Ref: (obj. 2, p. 532, Video)
5. D   Ref: (obj. 3, pp. 531-532)
6. D   Ref: (obj. 2, p. 534)
7. B   Ref: (obj. 2, p. 535)
8. A   Ref: (obj. 2, Video, Foner interview #1)
9.   Ref: (obj.3, Ch. 15, pp. 529-537 Video, Graff #1, Foner #1)
10.   Ref: (obj. 1, Ch. 16, pp. 529-537, Video, Graff #1)

Multiple-Choice

Select the single best answer. If more than one answer is required, it will be so indicated.

1. As the Allstons began to re-establish their lives after the Civil War, they found
    A. the world they knew could easily be re-established.
    B. new definitions for relationships would have to be established.
    C. the have-nots of society had now become the haves.
    D. it would be fairly simple to re-establish the old patterns of society.

2. As they became free, most slaves
    A. held great optimism for their future.
    B. wanted monetary compensation for their years of bondage.
    C. resisted the opportunity to change their lives.
    D. found ways to express their newfound freedom.

3. Professor Eric Foner said that the key element of disagreement between Congress and President Andrew Johnson was
    A. whether to disfranchise any Confederates.
    B. what to do with confiscated land.
    C. the status of the former slaves.
    D. the number of representatives to be allowed the states.

4. By the end of the Civil War, what seemed unclear to the nation?
    A. How to demobilize the Union and Confederate armies
    B. The economic condition of the North
    C. The place of the defeated southern states in the Union
    D. How to re-establish diplomatic contacts with Europe

5. After the war, Congress
    A. asserted its right to determine admission of states into the Union.
    B. allowed the executive branch to decide the postwar plans of the nation.
    C. found itself riddled by factions and unable to function.
    D. seemed unaware of the needs of the postwar nation.

6. The "black codes"
    A. provided freedmen with new political and civil opportunities.
    B. returned the freedmen to bondage.
    C. established a segregated society in the South.
    D. restricted the economic opportunities of the freedmen.

7. Andrew Johnson's plan for national reconstruction
    A. reflected his support for small southern yeoman farmers.
    B. called for harsh treatment of the South.
    C. stood staunchly on the side of the planter class.
    D. pleased the Republican leadership in Congress.

8. According to the Congressional Reconstruction Acts, a state to be readmitted had to do ALL of the following, EXCEPT
    A. write a state constitution which guaranteed black suffrage.
    B. allow women in the state to vote.
    C. ratify the Fourteenth Amendment.
    D. prohibit confederate leaders from participating in the political system.

Essay Questions

9. How did the goals of blacks and whites conflict in the South at the end of the Civil War?

10. Compare and contrast Lincoln's, Johnson's, and Congress's plans for Reconstruction. How were they alike, how were they different? Which do you believe was best for the majority of people? Explain.

FEEDBACK REPORT

1. B   Ref: (obj. 1, pp. 538-539)
2. D   Ref: (obj. 2, p. 543-544)
3. C   Ref: (obj. 3, Video, Foner interview #1)
4. C   Ref: (obj. 1, p. 540, Video)
5. A   Ref: (obj. 1, p. 541, Video)
6. D   Ref: (obj. 1, p. 546, Video)
7. A   Ref: (obj. 3, pp. 547-548, Video)
8. B   Ref: (obj. 4, p. 550, Video)
9.   Ref: (obj. 1 & 2, textbook Chapter 16, pp. 543-547, Video)
10.   Ref: (obj. 3, 4, pp. 547-550, Video, Foner int. #1, #2)

Multiple-Choice

Select the single best answer. If more than one answer is required, it will be so indicated.

1. Tenant farming and share cropping
    A. forced many blacks to migrate to the North.
    B. developed because of the freedmen's rejection of the contract labor system.
    C. changed very little the conditions of poor whites.
    D. reversed the relationship of planter and small farmer.

2. Reconstruction governments created under the Congressional plan
    A. were usually riddled with corruption and bribery.
    B. were ineffective in changing the structure of the South.
    C. built a solid political foundation for the Republican party.
    D. changed the role of state governments in the region.

3. Why did the Democrats return to power in the South?
    A. "Redeemer" politicians played upon the fears of southern society.
    B. The Republicans were uninterested in controlling the region.
    C. The Republicans had been unable to institute their program in the region.
    D. Freedmen grew disinterested in the political system.

4. The American public in the North (during the 1870s)
    A. strongly supported Congressional Reconstruction.
    B. believed the rights of blacks must be protected at all costs.
    C. grew increasingly disinterested in the South.
    D. believed the war had brought few changes.

5. The Grant administration can best be described as
    A. effective in providing national leadership.
    B. helpful in healing the wounds of the Civil War.
    C. a reflection of American society during this period.
    D. dominated by Redeemer political interests.

6. What major scandal of the Grant administration involved railroads and construction?
    A. Credit Mobilier
    B. Whiskey Ring
    C. Teapot Dome
    D. The Tweed Ring

7. Professor Eric Foner gave ALL of the following as reasons for the failure of radical-controlled southern government, EXCEPT
    A. the inherent weakness of those governments.
    B. the waning of northern support.
    C. racism in the north.
    D. Grant's refusal to support the governments.

Essay Question

8. How did the years of radical Reconstruction change the South? What were the most significant accomplishments of Reconstruction? What were the important failures? Overall, how would you rate the effectiveness of Reconstruction? Explain.

FEEDBACK REPORT

1. B   Ref: (obj. 1, p. 556)
2. D   Ref: (obj. 1, p. 561)
3. A   Ref: (obj. 2, p. 563, Video)
4. C   Ref: (obj. 2, p. 564, Video)
5. C   Ref: (obj. 2, p. 568)
6. A   Ref: (obj. 2, p. 568)
7. D   Ref: (obj. 3, Video, Foner interview #2)
8.   Ref: (obj. 1, textbook pp. 560-563, Video, Foner int. #2)